# My World Line

# George Gamow

———◆———

# My World Line

## AN INFORMAL

## AUTOBIOGRAPHY

Foreword by Stanislaw M. Ulam

———◆———

THE VIKING PRESS

NEW YORK

To my father and mother

# Foreword

*Fragments of Memory* was the title Gamow originally chose for his reminiscences, written over several years before his death on August 20, 1968. "Fragments" it turned out to be; his work is left unfinished in several ways. The chronological account ends with his arrival in the United States in 1934, covering less than half of his life, and there are only a few pages sketching the general character of his life and work in this country. There are also gaps in the narrative dealing with the earlier period. Gamow told me several times that he had planned to continue his autobiography but that upon reflection had decided against doing so, partly because he felt that an honest account of the events of recent times might offend various sensibilities. What a pity that his marvelous gift for succinct formulation and his ability to observe the essence of a matter through a mass of details were never brought to bear on scientific life here in the United States.

At the same time that he delighted in cutting through to the heart of things, Gamow kept track of all his activities in a very detailed and systematic way, which makes the omissions in the book seem the more unfortunate.

From the first time I met him, in 1936, I remember his collecting and putting in order all manner of snapshots and pictures of his various activities—markers, as it were, of scientific progress, vacation trips, discussions with friends—and his showing these with pride and pleasure to his guests. He also loved to compose photo-montages combining his own drawings with photographic cut-outs; these were intended as illustrations or caricatures of scientific discoveries. His collection of reprints of his own papers, as well as of the work of others which he considered especially interesting, was also very orderly.

All Gamow's writings are characterized by a natural flow of ideas, a simple uninvolved presentation of the material, and an easy, never redundant, amusing but never frivolous style. The reader will find that this book is no exception. Missing are the delightful misspellings of the manuscript itself. So typical of his writing, this trait has been much written about and discussed by his publishers. He wrote easily and quickly, hardly ever rewriting, filling innumerable pages, each with rather few lines handwritten in enormous characters.

His now classic books on the history of physics and on the new ideas in the physical sciences show his attitude toward fellow physicists to have been without malice or harsh judgment. He was sparing with real praise, reserving it for the very greatest achievements, but he never criticized, or even pointed out, mediocrity.

Gamow's popular books on science received great acclaim. For his contribution in popularizing physics, astronomy, and other natural sciences, he was awarded the UNESCO Kalinga Prize in 1956. I think one outstanding quality of these books is the simplicity of approach and the avoidance of unnecessary technical details that also distinguish his work in research. His honesty made him write exactly the way he thought—embodying the precept of Descartes: "ordering his thoughts to analyze the complex by dissecting it into its simpler parts."

In his scientific research Gamow was able to concentrate on certain problems over a period of many years, returning to the same questions time and again. A mathematician friend of mine, the late S. Banach, once told me, "The good mathematicians see analogies between theorems or theories; the very best see analogies between analogies." This ability to see analogies between models for physical theories Gamow possessed to an almost uncanny degree. In the present era of ever more complicated and perhaps oversophisticated use of mathematics, it was wonderful to see how far he could get with the use of intuitive pictures and analogies obtained by historical comparisons or even artistic ones.

Another characteristic of Gamow's work was the nature of the topics he dealt with; again, he never allowed his facility to carry him away from the mainstream of his subject in pursuit of unimportant details. It was in the great lines of the foundations of physics, in cosmology, and in the recent discoveries in biology that Gamow's ideas played such an important role. To give the reader just a few mere headings, we can point to his pioneering work in explaining the radioactive decay of atoms and on the explosive beginning of the universe and the subsequent formation of galaxies. (The recent discoveries of radiation pervading the universe and corresponding to a temperature of some 3 degrees absolute seem to confirm his prediction in 1948 concerning residual radiation from the Big Bang about 10 billion years ago.) After the discovery by Francis Crick and James Watson of the structure of the DNA molecule, Gamow was the first to suggest the existence in nature of a triplet code of four symbols governing the development of the life processes. In all, one may see in his work, among other outstanding traits, perhaps the last example of amateurism in scientific work on a grand scale.

This unfinished autobiography shows the same unassuming style and the same lack of conscious awareness of his great gifts, reflecting the totally natural ingenuousness of Gamow's reactions to the universe. An overwhelming curiosity about the scheme of things in nature—in the very large and in the very small—directed his work in nuclear physics and in cosmology. The origin, and perhaps the variability in time, of fundamental physical constants occupied his imagination and his efforts during the last years of his life. The great unanswered questions concern the relations between masses of elementary particles and also the very large numbers which are the ratios between the nuclear, electrical, and gravitational forces. Gamow thought that these numbers could not have arisen as a result of an initial accident, and that they might be obtainable from topological or number-theoretical considerations. He believed in the final simplicity of a theory which one day would explain these numbers.

In conversations during the last few months of his life he would return often to the consideration of schemata that might possibly throw light on this mystery. In a dream which he related to his wife shortly before his death, he had the tantalizing experience of being in the company of such great spirits as Newton and Einstein and of discovering, as they had discovered, the extreme simplicity of the ultimate scientific truths.

STANISLAW M. ULAM

*July 1969*

# Preface

All men of whatsoever quality they be who have done anything of excellence, or which may properly resemble excellence, ought, if they are persons of truth and honesty,
to describe their life with their own hands; but they
ought not to attempt so fine an enterprise till they have
passed the age of forty. This duty occurs to my own mind,
now that I am travelling beyond the term of fifty-eight
years, and am in Florence, the city of my birth. . . .

Oh no! Something has gone wrong. Today is my sixty-
fifth birthday, and I certainly was not born in Florence.

Oh, I see! I am just quoting the beginning of the autobiography of Benvenuto Cellini, translated into English
by John Addington Symonds.

However, it is a very nice beginning and would be very
suitable to any autobiography, so why not use it in mine?
To tell the truth, this book is, properly speaking, not a
regular, conventional autobiography. It is rather a collection of short stories, all of them pertaining to me, and all
of them completely true. But I will include only those stories which were interesting for me to write and therefore,
I believe, would be interesting for the reading public to

read. Thus the presentation is neither complete nor uniform. Many events and many periods of my life which may be of "considerable biographical importance" are simply omitted because I should have found it rather boring to describe them. Many omissions are made for purely personal reasons, the word "personal" meaning pertaining either to myself or to other persons. And about one-tenth of one per cent is omitted as pertaining to "classified" material.

Thus the contents of the book are mostly formed by stories which I would tell to a small company of friends after a good dinner and in front of a crackling fire—stories I enjoy telling and hope listeners will like to hear.

As for the title of the book, it refers to the relativistic four-dimensional space-time continuum in which anything that happens anywhere at any time is represented by a point. The sequence of such points (or events) forms a world line.

GEORGE GAMOW

*March 4, 1968*
*Boulder, Colorado*

# Contents

# My World Line

# I

## Childhood in Odessa

There is a mysterious spot in my genealogy; it seems that one of my great-great-granddaddies on the paternal side killed (in battle) one of my great-great-granddaddies on the maternal side, or vice versa.

The fact is that, according to some old documents which are now hopelessly lost, one of my paternal forebears was an officer in the Imperial Russian Army and was sent from St. Petersburg (now Leningrad) sometime early in the eighteenth century to liquidate the unruly Zaporozhets, Cossacks who lived on the Dnieper River islands between its rapids (*porogs*) and the Black Sea and formed a shield for the mother country by robbing and fighting Persians and Turks.

On my mother's side there is a long line of southern clergy who claimed descent from the Zaporozhets, and it is quite possible that one of my paternal forebears had to face one of my maternal ones on the field of battle.

My grandfather on the maternal side, Metropolitan Arseni Lebedinzev (the name was Russified from the original Ukrainian Lebedenez), was the chief priest of Odessa's cathedral and the religious administrator of Novorossia

3

—the lands located north of the Black and Azov Seas. He started his career as a priest in Sevastopol (in the Crimea). From 1854 to 1855 the city was besieged by the British and French Navies. The Russians lost, and the city had to be evacuated. My grandfather got instructions to come to a certain point on the embankment and wait for a navy

*Painting by Yevgeny Lansere of the Twelve Colleges (the Departments of War, Finance, the Interior, and so forth) built by Peter the Great in his new city, St. Petersburg. One of my paternal great-great-grandfathers may have been working in one of these buildings. Today the Twelve Colleges represent the spinal column of Leningrad University, in which I studied physics.*

*A group of Zaporozhes composing a letter to the Turkish Sultan (detail from a painting by Ilya Repin). One of my maternal great-great-grandfathers may have been among them.*

rowboat which would take him to the evacuation ship. He was there on time, with all his belongings: a bundle containing his clothes, a Bible, and a miracle-making icon. The icon was a very valuable one, made of pressed gold sheet, with openings cut in it to show the painted faces and hands of the Virgin Mary and the Child. The boat from the evacuation ship was delayed, and my grandfather stood there watching the British and French shells bursting in the air (while the Russian flag was still there!). Then something very unusual happened: my grandfather got an acute attack of diarrhea. There was a fence nearby, behind which he could go, but he was afraid to leave his belongings unattended. By chance, a young Russian sailor was passing by.

"Look, my boy," said my grandfather, "will you watch this bundle while I go behind this fence?"

"Certainly, Father," answered the sailor, and my granddaddy disappeared behind the fence.

Suddenly there was a big bang from one of the enemy's fragmentation shells, which burst right on the spot. When my grandfather rapidly pulled up his trousers and came out, he found the sailor dead and his bundle all ripped up and scattered. Only the holy icon remained unharmed, except that the fuse tube of the shell (a thin copper tube containing the primer detonating the main charge) got stuck in the hand of the Child.

Later on, when my grandfather became the Metropolitan, the icon, with the fuse tube still sticking from the hand, was attached to the wall of Odessa's cathedral, near the Holy Gates. I remember very well seeing it many times when I visited the cathedral as a child; the fuse tube became rather greenish because of the oxidation of the copper surface. I wonder if it is still there.

Metropolitan Arseni had four sons and one daughter. Only one of the sons, Uncle Vitia, chose a military career and became a commander of a battleship of the Black Sea Navy. Uncle Volodia became a chairman of Odessa's Court of Justice; Uncle Sasha, a schoolteacher of the Greek and Latin languages; and Uncle Senia graduated in chemistry from Odessa's university and worked on the chemistry of seas and lakes. He is credited with the discovery of the poisonous (for fish) carbon-compound layer at the bottom of the Black Sea. The Metropolitan's daughter, Alexandra (my mother), became a teacher of history and geography in one of Odessa's private schools for girls.

It is interesting to note here that Uncle Volodia's son Seva, whom I hardly remember because he was hanged when I was just a few years old, went to Italy to study astronomy with Professor Schiaparelli but got mixed up with a nihilistic group and came to St. Petersburg in an attempt to assassinate Prime Minister Stolypin. The attempt failed, and the five nihilists, along with two plain criminals, were "hanged by the neck until dead" at the estuary of the Neva. The story is nicely described in the book *The Seven Who Were Hanged* by Leonid Andreyev,[1] where my cousin is represented under the name "Unknown Who Called Himself Werner."[2] Of course the Russian secret police knew who he was, and at the next meeting of the Senate somebody raised the question: "What about that son of the Chairman of the Odessa District Court of Justice, who tried to assassinate the Prime Minister of Russia?" Fortunately, the President of the Senate was the godfather of my cousin. So he rose up and said, "I have investigated this question and found that it is a matter of mistaken identity. The case is closed." Thus Uncle Volodia retained his position until his death, and Aunt Nadia, his wife, received a good pension thereafter as long as the Czarist government lasted. After the 1917 Revolution her pension was of course canceled, but almost immediately she received another pension from the Soviet government for her son Seva, who had been executed because of his fight against the Czarist regime.

---

[1] Leonid Andreyev, *The Seven Who Were Hanged* (New York: J. S. Ogilvie, 1909).
[2] Actually he gave his name as Mario Calvino.

My paternal grandfather, Colonel Mikhail Gamow,[3] came to South Russia from the North as the commander of Kishinev's military district. He had four sons and one daughter. Three sons became Army officers and were killed in the Russo-Japanese War and in the World Wars I and II respectively. My aunt never married, and lived with the family of one of her officer brothers. But my grandfather could afford to send one of his sons, Anton (my father), to the University of Odessa, and he became a teacher of Russian language and literature in one of Odessa's private schools for boys. (In Russia, "school" then included not only high school but the freshman and sophomore college years of the American educational system.)

During his first year as a teacher, my father had a talented student named Lev Bronstein. The boy was the best in the class, and my father, who collected the papers of his best students, kept one of Bronstein's compositions for years. Unfortunately this document, along with many others collected during his long teaching career, was used to start a fire in our stove when there was a fuel shortage in the years of the Revolution.

On the other hand, Bronstein did not like my father and once organized a petition to the director of the school for his dismissal from his job. Being an excellent conspirator even at this young age, Lev Bronstein composed a petition which had as many words as there were students in the class, and each of the students wrote one word in his own handwriting. Nothing came of it, however, and my father retained his post.

[3] The correct pronunciation of this name is Gamov with *a* as in "mama" or "papa." If I had come from Russia straight to England or to the United States, I would have spelled my name in English with a *v* at the end. The *w*, confusing the issue, originated from the fact that I first spelled my name in the Latin alphabet for a publication in German, where *v* is pronounced like the English *f*, and *w* like English *v*.

Here is a passage from the autobiography [4] of this student of my father:

> In the upper grades the teaching of literature passed
> . . . to the hands of Gamov, who was still a young man,
> fair-haired, rather plump, very short-sighted, and without
> the least spark of interest in his subject. . . . To top this
> off, Gamov was also not punctual and would put off in-
> definitely the reviewing of our papers. In the fifth grade
> we were supposed to do four home papers on literature. I
> began to regard the task with an ever-growing attach-
> ment. I read not only the sources indicated by the
> teacher, but a number of other books as well, copying out
> facts and passages, altering and appropriating the sen-
> tences that caught my imagination, and in general work-
> ing with a great enthusiasm which did not always stop at
> the threshold of innocent plagiarism. There were a few
> other boys who did not regard composition merely as an
> odious task.

Quite a number of years later, my father met Lev on one of Odessa's boulevards, and in the course of the conversation asked him what he was doing.

"Oh, I am just working on the docks," was the answer.

"As a technician?"

Lev replied, "No, not quite." Little did my father know at that time with what kind of work his former best student was involved!

Now finally I come to myself. I was born in the Odessa apartment of my parents on the night of March 4, 1904, under very dangerous circumstances. I was too big and was wrongly located in my mother's womb, so that the concilium of doctors decided that on the next morning I

---

[4] Leon Trotsky's *My Life* (New York: Charles Scribner's Sons, 1930), p. 74. After joining the Communist Party, Bronstein changed his name to Trotsky, which was originally the stage name of his mother, a popular actress in Odessa theaters.

should be cut to pieces and extracted to save my mother's life. Fortunately for me, a woman living next door (who later became my godmother) knew that a well-known surgeon from Moscow (unfortunately I do not remember his name) was vacationing in a beach house belonging to one of her relatives, some ten or fifteen miles out of town. So in the middle of the night she got a horse and buggy, roused the surgeon from his bed, and brought him with his black bag to our apartment. The Caesarean section was performed on the writing desk in my father's study, where all the walls were lined with bookshelves. (This may be why I write so many books myself.)

A maid held a kerosene lamp, the neighbor woman (whom I always afterward called *Tetia-Mama*— "Auntie-Mama") sterilized the surgical instruments in the kitchen, and my father did what all other fathers do under such circumstances. Thus, thank you, I was born into this world.

By the age of seven, I was reading Jules Verne (or rather my mother was reading it to me), and I dreamed about a trip to the moon, a childish dream from which I am now completely cured. Even at this time I did some research in physics, trying to construct an electric bell by attaching an ordinary little bell (like the jingle bells on Santa Claus's reindeer) to an electric battery.

When I was nine years old my mother died, and so began Life with Father. My father was a devotee of the opera and often whistled or sang in half-voice arias from *Rigoletto, Faust, The Queen of Spades,* and so forth. He always insisted that I accompany him to the opera but never succeeded in getting me interested in it. Only once was I eager to go to the opera house, to see *Russlan and Ludmilla,* based on a fairy tale written by Pushkin, and composed by Glinka. In this story the Princess Ludmilla was stolen from her bridal bed by a black magician, Cher-

*My first summer on this earth. The photograph proves that I was a male child and that my father did not know (or was it intentional?) how to hold an infant in front of a camera.*

nomor. The distressed bridegroom, a famous knight named Russlan, went off to look for her. After many fantastic adventures he finally found Chernomor's magic castle and killed him, and they—Russlan and Ludmilla —lived happily ever after.

The reason I especially wanted to see, or more correctly

*At the Gamow dacha near Odessa in the summer of 1907.*

to hear, this opera was that during his long trip in search of his stolen bride Russlan encountered a giant's cut-off head which remained, however, quite alive. (Incidentally, I have not been able to find an English translation of *Russlan and Ludmilla,* although the shelves in the book-stores are piled high with many translations of *Eugene Onegin.* A pity!) This adventure occurs one evening when Russlan is riding through the vast steppe in search of his stolen bride. The pink sunset has faded and the new moon has risen in the sky. The steppe is still and foggy. Suddenly a hill looms large ahead of him, and Russlan hears loud snoring. His stallion refuses to move forward and shivers, with its mane erect. As the moon comes from behind the clouds, the hill becomes more visible. The brave knight sees a miracle before his eyes: to tease him, the giant's head has stuck out its fleshy red tongue. Furiously, Russlan casts his lance at the tongue, piercing it right in the middle. From the pain and astonishment the head nearly goes crazy trying to bite off the lance. Using this opportunity, Russlan gallops to the side of the head and delivers a powerful slap on its cheek with his iron-clad hand. As a result of the impact, the head falls down and rolls several times across the ground. At the place where it was originally located, Russlan now sees a large and shining magic sword, the only one capable of beheading the giant (as it did) and also of cutting the long beard of his brother, the magician Chernomor (the kidnaper of Ludmilla), which contains all his magic power. A long time before, Chernomor (who is smarter than his brother) cut off the giant's head and hid the sword under it, to make sure that nobody would get hold of it. With this sword in his hand, Russlan finally reaches Chernomor's castle and cuts off his long beard right under the chin. Thus he finally recovers his bride, and they live happily ever after.

As I have already remarked, my reason for going to this

particular opera was a desire to see the giant's head in all its glory. My father had taken a box in the *bel-étage,* at the right side of the opera house, but unfortunately the giant's head was located on the same side of the stage. When Russlan, riding a real black horse, appeared on the left side of the stage I could see him perfectly. But even though I leaned as far out of the box as I could, I still could not see the giant's head. I naturally burst into tears, and my father, spotting some friends in another, more favorably located box, grabbed me by the arm and we rushed over there. When we entered the friends' box, however, the curtain was just coming down, and all I could see was the very end of the beard of the giant's head.

In 1914 the World War started, and three years later came the Russian Revolution and the Civil War. By this time I was a schoolboy, but the schooling was very sporadic, since classes were often suspended when Odessa was bombarded by some enemy warships, or when Greek, French, or British expeditionary forces staged a bayonet attack along the main streets of the city against the entrenched, White, Red, or even green Russian forces, or when Russian forces of different colors fought one another.

In the meantime I was progressing in the arts and sciences, and I remember a day when I was reading a book on Euclidean geometry near a window in our apartment and the window pane was suddenly shattered by the shock wave of an artillery shell which exploded on the nearby street. Still, school life was going on, and I was getting more and more interested in astronomy and physics. Before the Revolution, and during the periods when Odessa was occupied by the White Army, classes in religion were as obligatory in all schools as were those in reading, 'rit-

ing, and 'rithmetic, and, being the grandson of a Metropolitan, naturally I had to be the best in the class. The
clergyman from the neighboring church who conducted
this class proudly called me the Deacon. But as I studied
the catechism and the order in which various prayers were
said and the psalms sung at the Easter service, I could not
help envying the Jewish boys, who were excused from
class and were playing ball in the schoolyard.

One day my father bought me a small microscope (the
five-and-ten-cent-store variety) and I decided to carry out
an important experiment in order to check the correctness
of the dogma. In the Russian Church during Commun-
ion, the red wine and the bread dropped into it turn into
the blood and flesh of our Savior, Jesus Christ. On one occasion, when the priest gave me an ounce of transubstan-
tiated wine and a crumb of bread on a gold-plated spoon,
I kept the piece of breadcrumb in my cheek, quickly ran
home, and put it under my microscope. For the sake of
comparison, I had earlier prepared a similar piece of
breadcrumb, soaked in red wine. Looking into my microscope, I could see no difference in the two specimens. The
texture of the two-pieces of bread was exactly the same,
and quite different from the texture of a tiny piece of my
skin which I cut from the end of my finger with a sharp
knife. The color of the sample I had taken home from
church was still reddish, but my microscope was not
strong enough to recognize individual erythrocytes. Thus
I had only a half-proof, but I think this was the experiment which made me a scientist.

Well, many things happened during these Revolutionary
years: Reds, Whites, Makhno, cholera, Reds again, German occupation, hunger, typhus, NEP (New Economic
Policy, introduced by Lenin), hunger again . . . But the
worst of all was the lack of water. The city of Odessa is located on the ridge of a plateau along the north shore of

the Black Sea, with an almost vertical drop of 150 feet to the water level. Down below is a narrow strip of land accommodating the piers, docks, storehouses, and other installations serving the marine trade across the Black Sea. Along the upper ridge runs a long boulevard with a beautiful view of the sea below and beyond. A broad flight of steps permitted people to go down to the seashore and to climb back up. Those readers who have seen the old Russian film *The Battleship Potemkin* may remember the broad flight of over a hundred steep steps which the dockworkers climbed to attack the city, under the fire of the police force from above. But these events took place during the unsuccessful Russian Revolution of 1905, and as at that time I was only a baby, I have no personal recollection of the event and must also draw my impressions from the film. My close acquaintance with the famous steps started some years later, when I was a pupil in an Odessa school.

Speaking historically, I can state that the city of Odessa was built by the Russian Empress Catherine the Great, late in the eighteenth century, after the Russian Army kicked out the Turks and Tartars occupying the northern shores of the Black Sea and annexed these lands to the Russian Empire. This region got the name of Novorossia (New Russia) and was colonized mostly by Ukrainians and some peasants from the North. There is a story that the French engineers of Catherine the Great advised her not to build a city at that place since, being 150 feet above sea level and not located on a river, it would not have a fresh water supply. But, as Catherine was a real empress who did not want to hear any arguments against her will, she said that there would be *assez d'eau* (plenty of water). Reading the French phrase backward, by syllables, one gets "eau-dzes-sa," which sounds like "Odessa," and so that became the name of the city. Of course this is nothing but

a legend and a *bon mot,* since it is well known that the
place was originally (in the fourth century) a Greek col-
ony called Odessus. But why not believe in the old fairy
tales?

The fact was, however, that the site of Odessa was dry
except for occasional rains, and the water had to be
brought from the Dniester River, located some twenty-five
miles away.

Alexander S. Pushkin wrote:

> In wet Odessa, tongues are clacking
> About an item that is lacking.
> Now *what* is lacking, do you think?
> *Sufficient water!* Just to drink
> Demands a maximum of labor
> From father, brother, uncle, neighbor.
> Odessans, never mind. Relax! . . .
> Wine is imported free of tax.[5]

Water was hauled daily to Odessa from the Dniester in
hundreds of horse-driven water-carts. Later, of course, a
long big-inch pipe was built to carry the water pumped to
Odessa by power plants located on the shores of the
Dniester. The pumps needed fuel, which was supplied by
coal mines in the Donezki region, hundreds of miles away.
Because of disruption of railroad communications, the
fuel often did not arrive on time, and the water pumps
stood idle. Some water was delivered to the docks at the
seashore, but the pressure was not high enough to lift the
water 150 feet up into the city. Thus to get some water, at
least for drinking and cooking (nobody cared about
bathing), the citizens of Odessa had to go down some
hundred steps to the docks, where water was weakly dripping from the public faucets. After about one hour of
waiting in line, one could finally fill up both buckets and
carry them 150 feet up into one's home. Being at that

[5] Odessa was a free port.

time a young and strong boy, I did this daily, which took
considerable time from my studies. One day, standing in
line, I got into a conversation with a sailor from a British
destroyer which was docked close to the water faucet.
"W'at's hit all abaout?" he asked. "I need some water,"
I answered in my poor English. "Come 'ere, lad," said the
sailor, who led me to the destroyer's side, produced a
water hose, and filled my two buckets in a few seconds. At
this sight, the entire line of Odessa's thirsty citizens followed me, and the sailor of His Majesty's Navy obligingly
filled all their buckets too. Blessing the British Navy, we
carried the precious water up the long flight of steps to
our homes. But we were in for a shocking surprise: the
water was plain salt water from Odessa's bay. After this incident I began to appreciate the British sense of humor.

Another problem was of course bread, which was very
scarce and heavily rationed. But here another occupation
power came to our rescue. The French Moroccan forces,
which had to evacuate Odessa in a hurry, left behind a
large amount of food for their mules; I do not know
enough botany to give it a name. Next day this "grain"
was delivered to Odessa's bakeries to be made into bread
for the starving population. The supply was plentiful and
everyone in line got a big loaf of "French bread." It
turned out, however, to be quite uneatable—except
perhaps by the mules. In spite of all this hardship, the
Odessans did not lose their sense of humor and composed
the following verse:

> The dough of Baker Bosch is
> Such delicious, thin dough,
> It serves to mend galoshes
> Or putty up a window.

Finally there was the problem of fuel for heating houses
and cooking food. The north shore of the Black Sea is
steppe—covered with grass but completely lacking in

any wooded areas. The trees lining Odessa's boulevard and in the beautiful parks were planted when the city was founded, and Odessa was all green with majestic acacias which filled the air with aroma when they were in bloom. All these trees were cut down for fuel (as were many old wooden buildings), and the city looked naked and color-less. Said the French mathematician Lagrange when, during the French Revolution, the head of the famous chemist Lavoisier was chopped off on the guillotine: "It took a moment to chop off this head, but perhaps a century will not be sufficient to produce an equal one." I have not been in Odessa for several decades, and thus cannot report on its present-day flora.

One more remark concerning the food situation. There was hunger in the cities but not in the food-producing villages, and the peasants hoarded and hid food. One way to get some bread and butter, or maybe a chicken, was to walk to a village not too far from the city, carrying along some silk handkerchiefs, a few pieces of family silver, or even a golden watch, and to exchange these for food. Many enterprising city inhabitants did this, even though it was a dangerous undertaking.

Here is a story told to me by one of my friends who was at that time a young professor of physics in Odessa. His name was Igor Tamm (Nobel Prize laureate in Physics, 1958). Once when he arrived in a neighboring village, at the period when Odessa was occupied by the Reds, and was negotiating with a villager as to how many chickens he could get for half a dozen silver spoons, the village was captured by one of the Makhno bands, who were roaming the country, harassing the Reds. Seeing his city clothes (or what was left of them), the capturers brought him to the Ataman, a bearded fellow in a tall black fur hat with machine-gun cartridge ribbons crossed on his broad chest and a couple of hand grenades hanging on the belt.

"You son-of-a-bitch, you Communistic agitator, undermining our Mother Ukraine! The punishment is death."

"But no," answered Tamm, "I am a professor at the University of Odessa and have come here only to get some food."

"Rubbish!" retorted the leader. "What kind of professor are you?"

"I teach mathematics."

"Mathematics?" said the Ataman. "All right! Then give me an estimate of the error one makes by cutting off Maclaurin's series at the $n^{th}$ term. Do this, and you will go free. Fail, and you will be shot!"

Tamm could not believe his ears, since this problem belongs to a rather special branch of higher mathematics. With a shaking hand, and under the muzzle of the gun, he managed to work out the solution and handed it to the Ataman.

"Correct!" said the Ataman. "Now I see that you really are a professor. Go home!"

Who was this man? No one will ever know. If he was not killed later on, he may well be lecturing now on higher mathematics in some Ukrainian university.

While studying mathematics and physics in school, I was also spending some time reading Russian literature, mostly poetry rather than prose, because the former sounded much better and also is not so long. (Compare the number of words in *Eugene Onegin* with that in *War and Peace!*)

I have a very poor memory when it comes to names or numbers. But somehow after a few readings of a verse, even a rather long one, I remember it for an indefinite period of time. Several years ago I visited some Russian friends in San Diego and made a bet that I could quote Russian verses from memory for at least one hour, nonstop. I won the bet, quoting verses for an hour and a half, and stopped not because I ran out of verses but because the audience got tired. The next day I got my punishment in the form of laryngitis, which forced me to cancel my lecture that night.

From early childhood I still remember such verses as:

> Ding dong bell! Ding dong bell!
> Fire in kitty's house I smell.
> Hen brings water from the well.
> Flames to quell! Ding dong bell!

And:

> Birdie, birdie, where were you?
> On Fontanka all night through,
> Drinking vodka—one glass, two . . .
> Till my tongue was thick as glue.

At school age I turned to more serious poetry, and I should like to quote here, and later in the book, some passages, not so much to demonstrate my memory but rather because they pertain to various historical events, personal and political. Making the selection, I found that only a few verses I wanted to quote had been rendered into English. Many others had been printed in the original Russian but never translated, while most of them had never even been printed and were just circulating around, their authorship unknown. Thus I asked my wife, Barbara, who is an American, to help me with this task. I dictated the verses to her, translating from Russian into English, and she put them into English verse. All the verses the reader encounters in this book which do not carry a reference to the author and translator were produced that way.

The following poem, written by Alexander Blok in 1918, pertains to the early stages of the Russian Revolution, showing some of its various aspects.

THE TWELVE [6]

*by Alexander Blok*

(English version by Anselm Hollo)

Black night
Snow falls
Wind wind
No one can stand against it
Strews
Flakes white
Ice beneath
Slip fall
This happens to all
Poor bastards
. . . .

Snow dance
Spray whirl
Flames glare
Snow
Walk on
The Twelve walk on
Battered caps
Soggy spud
Look like jailbirds
Freedom Freedom Freedom
No crucifixes here

Hey

Cold bitter
Cold
. . . .

That's where they've gone baby yes that's where they've
    gone
Gone to join the Red Guard yes gone to join the Red
    Guard

[6] This appeared in the *Evergreen Review*, Vol. 5, No. 19 (July–August
1961).

Oh the reds and the blues oh
Yes the reds and the blues
Yes you need rags to cover your bones
Oh yes you need rags to cover your bones
And a dead man's gun
Yes and a dead man's gun.

We'll set the world on fire they say
That's our mad desire they say
We'll set all that blood on fire they say
All that blood running in the streets
All that blood God all that blood
          . . . .

You never heard of our Revolution or what
Keep in step man keep in step
Don't think the bastards gone to sleep
We got to keep on walking yes
We got to keep on walking
And they keep on walking and they have no name
And they are the Twelve
And they can take it and they are going to make it
They are going to make it new

Their rifles are shiny
The barrels are steel
But the streets are empty
The streets end nowhere
The streets end in snow
In deserts of snow
And oceans of snow

Red flag
Rattles
Keep in step

And their enemy is on the march
And their enemy is on the move
And the wind keeps on hitting them hard
Hitting them when the sun is up
Hitting them when the sun is down

Got to keep on walking peoples
Got to keep on walking!

By the time I finished school the Civil War was over,
the remnants of the White Army were evacuated from the
Crimea to Turkey, and the fighting (except for the so-
called bandit groups) had stopped.

I enrolled at Novorossia University in Odessa in the
physico-mathematical faculty.[7] The university was just re-
covering from the disasters of the Revolution and the
Civil War, and was to a large extent non-operative. There
was a strong group of mathematicians: Professor Shchatunovski, who lectured in higher algebra; Professor Kagan,
who lectured in multi-dimensional geometry; and a
younger man, Professor Yuri Rabinovich, whose main interest was in the theory of relativity. Those are the three
men who gave me my taste for mathematics. I remember
that once during class Shchatunovski asked a student the
question: "If you multiply five cab-drivers by three can-
dlesticks what do you get?" The student was embarrassed
and made no answer. "Well," said Shchatunovski, "it will
be fifteen cab-driver-candlesticks." This gave me for the
first time the basic idea of Dimensional Analysis and influenced my future work in science.

Another time Shchatunovski made an arithmetical mistake on the blackboard, writing:

$$37 \times 25 = 837$$

When a student remarked that he thought the correct answer would be 925, Shchatunovski exploded. "It is not the
job of mathematicians," he snapped, "to do correct arithmetical operations. It is the job of bank accountants."
This remark made a deep impression on me, and even
today I am not ashamed if in multiplying $7 \times 8$, I get 45.

[7] Officially the university was called not "the University of Odessa," but
Novorossia University. This name pertained to a large region of Russia
with that name, north of the Black Sea, centered in Odessa.

*The main entrance of Novorossia University in Odessa.*

The lectures of Professor Kagan were scheduled in the evenings, and the trouble was that the classrooms were not illuminated. Owing to the shortage of fuel, the electric power was often cut off. But nevertheless he continued to hold his classes, arguing that, anyway, multidimensional figures could not be drawn on a two-dimensional blackboard.

The students and the professor himself had to climb an iron fence surrounding the campus (on the nights when there was no power the janitors went off duty early, so there was nobody to open the gates), and we traveled through the corridors of the university building, lighting our way with matches. But, nevertheless, the small group who went through these adventures got excellent grades on the final examination. "This proved," Professor Kagan pointed out, "that imagination is vastly superior to illumination."

Professor Yuri Rabinovich, the youngest of the teaching staff, was the keeper of the *Cabchismat* (the Cabinet of Pure Mathematics), where we could read books and magazines during the daytime and also chatter about mathematics and many other things by night. He managed to escape abroad soon after I enrolled at the university, and the next time I met him, during one of my visits to Ann Arbor, he was called Professor Y. Reinich of the University of Michigan. Needless to say, we spent that day in pleasant reminiscences.

But there were no physics lectures in Novorossia University. Professor Kasterin, the head of the department, refused to lecture, on the grounds that he could not get an assistant to arrange the demonstrations for his lectures. These would have been impossible anyway because of the complete absence of supplies for the demonstrations— whether of Galileo's experiment with the pendulum or J. J. Thomson's experiments with the electron beam.

"I do not want to give 'melodramatic lectures,' " he declared at the faculty meeting. This was a play on words, since in Russian *mel* means "chalk" (in Greek, *melo* means "black"), and all he meant was that he did not want to lecture just using chalk (which also was often absent) on the blackboard, without demonstrations.

Actually I did not meet Professor Kasterin until many years later, but I was very well acquainted with his daughter Tatiana (Tanya for short), who was a student in my class; in fact, Tanya and I became very good friends and could have become husband and wife had I not been so shy. But I was shy, so nothing came of it.

After a year in the university, I decided to leave my native city and go to Leningrad (Petrograd at that time), where, as I heard, physics had started to flourish again after its hibernation during the Revolutionary period. Of course this was not an easy step.

My father sold most of our family silver to provide me with some money for the trip, and I left Odessa.

# 2

## University Days in Leningrad

In Leningrad I had only one connection, Professor Obolenski, who earlier had been a colleague of my father in
Odessa's high school, but then became a professor of meteorology in Leningrad's Forestry Institute. When I came
to him, he offered me the job of an observer at the institute's meteorological station—a job requiring comparatively short hours (6:00 a.m. to 6:20 a.m.; 12:00 noon to
12:20 p.m.; and 6:00 p.m. to 6:20 p.m., including Satur-
days and Sundays). I had to take readings of maximal and
minimal thermometers, measure the direction and force of
the wind, check the barometric pressure, and a few other
things. These "few other things" were often rather uncom-
fortable. For example, there were a number of thermometers installed at different heights in the shrubbery patches,
and I had to take readings three times a day. I still remember climbing on my knees (with a flashlight, before
or after sunset, during the winter months) with snow falling on my head. But $3 \times 20$ minutes $= 1$ hour per day, and
the job left me enough time to attend the university lectures and to read scientific books and magazines.

A few years later I came in conflict with Professor Obolenski, who wanted me to become an experimental meteorologist, while I wanted to become a theoretical physicist. Thus I had to leave his laboratory, but was lucky enough to get the job of colonel in the Red Army Field Artillery School. Of course, to become a colonel at the age of twenty sounds somewhat fantastic, but it was really the case. The point was that I got a job as a lecturer in physics in the Artillery School of the Red October (formerly the Artillery School of the Grand Duke Konstantin), and, according to the regulations existing at that time (which may still exist today), was given a military rank corresponding to my salary. It was equal to a field army colonel's salary, so I got a colonel's uniform. Unfortunately I have lost the photograph of myself with all the army regalia, attending a meeting of Leningrad's Physical Society, but the uniform was truly beautiful: a gray tunic with red-bordered black crossbars and two red stars on the sleeves; four squares indicated the rank of colonel. But the squares were blue rather than red, indicating that I was not a fighting man but was connected with non-combatant activities. The shining black riding boots with spurs and an *umootvod* (conical hat) with a red star completed the outfit.

During the winter months I taught cadets the elements of physics and meteorology, but in the summer, when the school went to the shooting ground at Luga, not far from Leningrad, I got a new job. I became a commander of the "meteorology group," comprised of a dozen cadets and a horse-driven carriage carrying the theodolites, rubber balloons, and hydrogen cylinders for estimating the direction and strength of the wind.

According to my rank, I was also entitled to my own horse, a large black animal, Voron (or "Raven" in English), who was able to carry my weight. This was the first time I had ever mounted a horse. When, with some difficulty, I climbed into the saddle in the camp stable, Voron refused to move, and the Red Army soldiers tending the stables roared with laughter watching my efforts to use the spurs. I dismounted and pulled the horse by the bridle some distance out of the camp. And then, although I do not know how I did it, I jumped into the saddle! Voron turned around and trotted back into the stable, to the loud applause of the soldiers.

The next day I made a friend, whose name I do not remember, but if he ever happens to read these lines I want to send him my best regards and gratitude. He was a veteran of many battles in the Civil War, one of the many who were retained in the Red Army as teachers of the art of fighting. He took me to the stables and selected for me another horse, called Cavaleria ("Cavalry" in English). It was a small black and white spotted horse that was used for *voltigirovka*—the exercise in which soldiers jump up on the horse while it is running at full gallop, lean down from the saddle to pick up with their teeth a handkerchief dropped on the ground, and perform other acrobatics. Cavaleria became a friend of mine at first sight, despite the disproportion in our sizes and the fact that when I rode her my boots almost dragged on the ground. This prompted in the camp's *Sten-gazeta* (lithographed daily sheet) a drawing of me riding this horse with the caption: "Jesus Christ on a Donkey." In any case, this is how I learned the art of horseback-riding, even though I never graduated to mastering the Western saddle, which never gave me anything but a spanking.

The summer in Luga was very exciting, and my newly acquired friend taught me many tricks. During maneuvers I used to ride side by side with him in front of the cavalry squadron, some hundred mounted soldiers riding in close formation (*lava* we call it in Russian) behind us. Once we had to cross an open field, supposedly under the enemy's artillery fire. "Gallop!" came the command, and the horses rushed forward as fast as they could. Somehow my right foot got out of the stirrup. I managed not to fall from the saddle under the hoofs of the onrushing horses, but hung with my knee over the saddle, holding the horse's mane with my left hand. Suddenly the strong hand of one of the horsemen, who galloped up from behind, grabbed my collar and put me back in the saddle. Since that summer in Luga I can say that I can ride horses, provided they are equipped with MacLean-type saddles.

A most exciting experience that summer took place on a day when the commander of a trigonometrical group became sick and I was ordered to take it, too, under my command. There were two groups attached to the Artillery School: one, trigonometrical, whose job was to measure the azimuths and ranges of targets; and the other, meteorological, whose job was to make corrections for the wind, the temperature of the gunpowder, and so forth. The shooting ground was a hilly, wooded area with many lakes, and the targets were usually two-dimensional churches, like stage props—partially for convenience in aiming, partially as anti-religious propaganda. I saw seven churches, and I ordered the trigonometrical group to get their exact positions. Then the boys of my own group introduced the wind corrections, and I galloped to the hill on which the division commander and his staff were stationed, and handed him the list of targets. Field officers in communication with the batteries hidden in the woods started giving information for aiming, but then a very fortunate thing happened. A supervisor, permanently attached to the shooting field, glanced through the list and asked me, "How is it you have *seven* churches?"

"Well," I answered, "one here, another there, . . . and the seventh over there."

"But hell!" he shouted. "The seventh is *not* a target but

Saint Nicholas Church in the village across the road."

"Hold the fire on target seven!" roared the division commander into his microphone. "Hold the fire on target seven!" echoed the officer in the field. This saved the lives of a few hundred peasants who were attending morning mass in Saint Nicholas Church.

And this finished my adventure with the Red Army, which, however, had some reverberations many years later—to be exact, in 1949. Being at that time a professor of physics at George Washington University in Washington, D.C., I was invited to spend my sabbatical year at the Los Alamos Scientific Laboratory of the Atomic Energy Commission in New Mexico. I was already a United States citizen when the so-called Manhattan Project was organized to produce the A-bomb, but was at that time refused clearance to work on it because of information in the security office to the effect that I had once served as a colonel in the Red Army.

But by 1949, when President Truman said yes to the development of the H-bomb, I was sufficiently cleared to go to Los Alamos to help with the problems of thermonuclear weapons. Everything went well, and after four months there I went for a two-week summer vacation to Malibu Beach in California. After a hard drive I arrived in Malibu Beach in the afternoon and found a very nice motel to stay in. I put on my swimming trunks and was waist-deep in the water, looking forward to a nice swim, when the motel manager and two tough-looking characters appeared on the beach, shouting to me to come back. The two men presented me with their identification cards (one AEC Security, and the other FBI) and told me that they had been combing the motels along the beach all day long and were happy to have found me in time.

"What's your hurry?" I asked, and found that I was to

call Dr. Norris Bradbury, the Director of Los Alamos Laboratory, right away. When I lifted the receiver, the water still dripping from my swimming trunks, I heard Norris's voice.

"Sorry to disturb you, George," he said, "but you must be back here tonight. If you hurry, you can still make the last plane from Los Angeles to Albuquerque, and take the Carco plane taxi here. I will tell you what it is about after you arrive."

The two agents helped me to get out of my wet swimming suit and into dry, presentable clothes, and we rushed, with the siren screaming, to the airport, and arrived just a few minutes before the plane took off. All the way I was very excited, dreaming that there must be some important job for which I was indispensable.

When later that day I stepped into Bradbury's office, I found there another man, Captain Smith, the Director of Security, affectionately known to all Los Alamites as "Smitty." They explained to me that tomorrow morning there would be a hearing in Washington, at which Senator McCarthy was going to accuse the AEC of insufficient security precautions. One of the accusations that Senator McCarthy was going to make was that in inviting me to Los Alamos the Commission did not get sufficient information about my military connections with other countries.

"Here," said Smitty, holding out a questionnaire, "is a paragraph asking whether or not you have served in the military forces of any other country. If the answer is yes, you have to specify details."

"The answer is yes," I said. "I was a colonel in the field artillery of the Red Army."

Smitty put his fingers into his ears and murmured, "I didn't hear it! I didn't hear it!"

When I gave more details about the innocuous nature

of my "military" career, an urgent and reassuring telephone call went to the AEC Security Officer in Washington, and Norris, Smitty, and I then had a nice drink toast-
ing Senator McCarthy. The next afternoon I finally
plunged into the waters of the Pacific, and a fortnight
later landed back at my desk in Los Alamos.

While teaching at the Artillery School I attended classes
at the university, and by the spring of 1925 I had passed
all examinations required for a Diploma. It may be
noted here that Russian as well as most European universities have rigid programs and if one selects a given field
such as mathematics, optics, or electricity, one *must* attend
the lectures and pass all examinations listed in the selected program. This stands in contrast to the American
system, where, for example, a student majoring in physics
may attend a class in Greek history and get credit for
it. Of course, students were not prohibited from attending other classes, but they got no credit for it. The grades
given at the examinations were: "Good," "Satisfactory,"
and "Failure." And those whose grades were all "Good"
stood a chance of becoming "aspirants"—that is, proposed to start work toward the Ph.D., and automatically
entitled to a stipend. A student could not apply to become an aspirant but had to be proposed by a professor,
just as in the United States and elsewhere girls do not ask
boys to marry them but wait until the men make the proposal. Of course, there are ways in which a girl can induce
the desired man to make the proposal, and Russian students used similar methods with their professors. I was the
protégé of Professor Dmitri Rogdestvenski, affectionately
called Uncle Mitya, who was the Director of the Physics
Institute and was working in the field of optics. When I
"finished" the university (passed all the required examinations with the grade "Good"), Professor Rogdestvenski

told me that he considered me an "aspirant" but recom-
mended that I wait for one year. The point was that I finished the university one year earlier than I should have
according to the program (in three years instead of four)
so that, if he presented my name to the selection committee I would be competing with older students who had
been in the university the full four years, and because the
number of "aspirantships" was limited, I would have less
chance to be selected. I told him that this would be quite
all right with me, except that I had to find a new job for
that year to get some money for food and lodging.[1] My
work in the Artillery School was only temporary; I was
substituting for the regular teacher of physics, who was on
leave of absence for one year and was coming back.

"That is easy to arrange," said Uncle Mitya. "I will give
you a job for that year in the state's Optical Institute"—
GOI for short.

GOI was a new research institute, one of the great
many established by the Soviet government after it began
to realize the importance of science. The building was
side by side with the university's Physics Institute, and
Professor Rogdestvenski was the director of both. The
name of the institute led to a number of jokes, based on
the fact that it sounded (and in Russian it was also
spelled) exactly like the Yiddish word *goy*, a somewhat
disdainful name for a Christian. It corresponded to reality
because there was only one Jewish employee there, perhaps because the name of the director was derived from
the Russian word *Rogdestvo*, which means Christmas. On
the other hand, another new physics laboratory known as
the Roentgen Institute, which was connected with the Poly-
technical Institute and organized and directed by the
noted professor Abraham Joffe, had a very meager Christian population.

[1] There was then no tuition fee in the Soviet universities.

The work I had to do in GOI was not very exciting and rather technical. When one cooks glass for high-precision optical instruments one selects only a small fraction of the product, the part which is absolutely homogeneous and contains no schlieren (a German word also used in English), which are the veins of glass of a somewhat higher or lower density running through the irregular glass blocks some 30 cubic feet in volume as they come from the glass-cooking furnaces. Of course you cannot see the schlieren in them because of the roughness and irregularity of the surface.

My job was to develop a method of seeing the schlieren so that the good pieces of glass could be cut out by a pneumatic hammer. The idea was to place the glass block into a large glass container resembling an aquarium and to fill this up with a liquid which had exactly the same refractivity as the sample of glass in question. When this is done, light rays are not refracted as they pass through the interface between the glass block and the surrounding fluid, and the block becomes practically invisible, more or less as a jellyfish is when floating in water. The liquid was a mixture of Canadian balsam and some other liquid, the name of which I have forgotten; when these are combined in correct proportion, one can fit the refractivity of the fluid to that of any kind of glass. Then the schlieren became visible, and, plunging the pneumatic hammer into the aquarium, one could chip off the good clear pieces from which lenses would be made. Though I was more interested in the quantum theory than in glass-cracking, I started enthusiastically on the project and cut a number of good glass fragments, much better (in my opinion) than ordinary window glass. Maybe the lenses made of them still sit in some old Russian theodolites.

Professor Rogdestvenski also suggested that, along with this bread-and-butter job, I start, before becoming offi-

*At the University of Leningrad in 1925: Professor Rog-destvenski (at left) greets the Indian physicist Sir Van-kata Raman (center), with the author, a graduate stu-dent, standing behind Raman to the right.*

cially an aspirant, the research which I should do the fol-lowing year. It was in the field of physical optics and in-volved the study of abnormal changes in the refractivity of gases in the neighborhood of absorption lines, by using the so-called "hook method" which he had invented a few years ago. Thus I got my own room in the Physics Insti-tute, which was filled with piles of sensitive optical instru-ments. I will not bore the reader with the principles and methodology of these experiments, and will mention only the so-called "interferometer," consisting of two half-sil-vered glass plates which must be kept parallel with the

precision of one-millionth of an inch. After adjusting
them with great labor, one sneezes and everything comes
out of adjustment! I called them the entrance-and-exit
devils.

This was the time when I first tasted vodka. Before the
Revolution I had been too young to use liquor, and during
World War I the Prohibition Law was introduced. But
in my workroom I had a gallon of pure alcohol (equivalent to 200-proof vodka), which was necessary for sensitiz-
ing the photographic plates used in taking the infrared
spectra. One day I decided to see how vodka tastes. Using
a graduated cylinder, I put in the proper proportions of
pure alcohol and distilled water, and, after mixing them
with a glass stick, drank the mixture to the bottom. It did
not taste very good, and I did not feel anything. I repeated the experiment, but with the same negative result,
except that I felt I would like some food. Since it was
lunchtime anyway, I decided to go to the university's dining room. When I passed through the door of my laboratory room, I noticed that there was something wrong with
the corridor floor: it was buckling and bending as if there
were an earthquake. However, balancing myself like a
sailor on a rocking ship, I reached the dining room and
ate a good lunch by Russian standards of that time. On
my way back to the physics building, the sea quieted
down considerably.

Another time I availed myself of the liquid from that
bottle, it was not for interior but rather for exterior pur-
poses. In the winter Leningrad becomes awfully cold and
the great river Neva covers itself with a thick layer of ice.
You may hire a horse-drawn sled and tell the *kutscher*
(driver) to drive you onto the frozen river at one of the
boat embarkments and along a mile or so to the next one,
where there is another set of steps. It happened that, although I lived directly across the river from the univer-

sity, it was a long walk far to the right to get to one
bridge, or far to the left to get to another. But in the winter I could walk as the crow flies, just crossing the frozen
Neva from shore to shore.

Of course, there were streetcars to the bridges, but they
were very inconvenient and even dangerous to the health.
First of all, they were terribly crowded; the people were
packed thickly in the central passage and on the front and
back platforms. Those who could not enter the car hung
outside with one foot on the step, holding on to the hand-
bars, and the danger was that they would collide with another bunch of "outside passengers" hanging on a streetcar going in the opposite direction. No, I do not mix my
geometry; when a Russian streetcar came to a stop it was
attacked by the prospective passengers from both sides. I
hope this is not so now. The medical danger arose from
the fact that a large number of passengers had lice, often
infected with the typhus virus, crawling around in their
clothes. In crowded places the lice migrated from person to person, with unpleasant consequences. Thus, I
walked.

But to come back to the main line of the story, I must
relate an incident that occurred once while I was crossing
the frozen Neva early in the spring as the ice began to
melt. When I came to the university side of the river, I
saw a strip of water stretching between the safe ice surface
and the snow-covered steps. There was no way to say
whether it was water covering a thick ice layer below, or
whether there was no ice layer below at all. Anyway, the
water strip was only a foot or so wide, and I decided to
jump. My feet touched the steps, but I slipped on the
snow and plunged back into the icy water almost up to
the shoulders. Fortunately I managed to grab the lowest
step with one hand, and a few men standing there (probably also trying to decide whether or not to jump) pulled

me out. All wet and dripping, I walked to the physics
building, just five minutes away, took off all my clothes,
and hung them near the electric heater which I was using
to dry negatives. But my main concern was my wrist-
watch, which of course was not waterproof. Wrist-watches
were as rare in Russia as fountain pens, caviar, and other
luxuries. I poured out a full glass of pure alcohol and put
my wrist-watch into it. Enough alcohol was left for me to
repeat my earlier experiment, mixing it with water and
taking it internally. As a result, my wrist-watch started
tick-tocking again after drying, and I escaped pneumonia.

But somehow my spectroscopic work did not progress

*View across the Neva River in Leningrad: from left to
right, the university buildings (compare painting on
page 4); the Academies of Sciences; and the "needle" of
the Admiralty. In the foreground at right is the monu-
ment to Peter the Great. (The steps leading down to the
water where I fell through the ice are to the right of the
university buildings.)*

too well. The photographs of the spectra were mostly out of focus and underdeveloped, the latter defect being due to the fact that I used the development-intervals from a book where they were given for room temperature (70 degrees Fahrenheit), while, because of the fuel shortage, the temperature of the laboratories was usually below 50 degrees. Of course, any good experimentalist would have taken this into account, knowing that the rate of most chemical reactions changes by a factor of 2 when the temperature changes by 20 degrees Fahrenheit; but even though I knew that, I did not think about it.

All these mishaps with my experimental work finally persuaded me that it takes more than a desire to have one's own room in the institute to become an experimental physicist, and I also realized the futility of my plan to be half experimentalist and half theoretician.

The subject which fascinated me most from my early student days was Einstein's special, and especially general, theory of relativity, and I had quite a lot of somewhat uncoordinated knowledge in this field. What I needed most at that time was a strict mathematical foundation in the field. It just happened that Professor Alexander Alexandrovich Friedmann of the Mathematics Department announced at that time his course of lectures entitled "Mathematical Foundations of the Theory of Relativity," and so, naturally, I landed on the bench of the classroom for the first of his lectures. Friedmann, who was basically a pure mathematician, also had a vast interest in the application of mathematics in various branches of the physical sciences, and at this time was involved in the project of the development of detailed hydrodynamics of the atmosphere. Being well ahead of his time, he planned to study a "cube of air," that is, a large volume of terrestrial atmosphere, the detailed physical conditions within which were to be measured by a fleet of manned and unmanned bal-

loons, released from various locations at the base of the region in question. But he was also excited by the problems
of relativistic cosmology and had become the originator of
the theory of the expanding universe. Since his exact role
in that theory is unknown to most of today's researchers,
whereas I have it at first hand, directly from him, I am
going to tell it here in some detail.

When in 1915 Einstein formulated his famous equation

*Professor Alexander A. Friedmann.*

of general relativity and applied it successfully to the explanation of the long-existing discrepancy in the perihelion motion of Mercury, the deflection of light rays in the gravitational field of the sun, and the gravitational red shift of the lines in the solar spectrum, he decided to use the theory for the description of the universe as a whole.

It was the great Sir Isaac Newton, the discoverer of the Law of Universal Gravity, who was the first to worry about the stability of the cosmos. If each piece of matter in the universe attracts each other piece by the forces of gravity, why hasn't the entire universe collapsed into a pulp? Einstein thought that his improved theory of gravity could deal successfully with Newton's old paradox, and so secure the stability of the cosmos. As the first step, Einstein devised a mathematical argument which seemed to prove that, in spite of Newton's fears, the universe could be stable, with all its masses staying put in their original positions. Then he proceeded to find the distribution of masses which would lead to such a stable universe unchangeable in time. But in doing so he ran into an unexpected difficulty: there was no possible distribution of masses that would satisfy the condition of stability. It was a logical paradox of the type:

A) If the universe exists, it must be stable.

B) There can be no stable universe.

Hence:

A+B) The universe does not exist.

Well, Einstein did not go that far, and simply concluded that the basic equation of general relativity was incorrect in application to the universe and had to be changed. In fact, he had found that the situation could be helped, and the universe saved from ultimate collapse, if his original equation were augmented by the addition of one more term, which became known as the "cosmological term." True, the new term had a rather strange physical interpretation, representing a repulsive force which increases with the distance between the two objects and depends on the mass of only one of them. But nothing was too much to save the universe! This resulted in the famous Einstein model of a stable spherical universe, introduced by him in 1917.

Studying Einstein's publications on that subject from a purely mathematical point of view, Friedmann noticed that Einstein had made a mistake in his alleged proof that the universe must necessarily be stable and unchangeable in time. It is well known to students of high-school algebra that it is permissible to divide both sides of an equation by any quantity, provided that this quantity is not zero. However, in the course of his proof, Einstein had divided both sides of one of his intermediate equations by a complicated expression which, in certain circumstances, could become zero.

In the case, however, when this expression becomes equal to zero, Einstein's proof does not hold, and Friedmann realized that this opened an entire new world of time-dependent universes: expanding, collapsing, and pulsating ones. Thus, Einstein's original gravity equation was correct, and changing it was a mistake. Much later, when I was discussing cosmological problems with Einstein, he remarked that the introduction of the cosmological term was the biggest blunder he ever made in his life. But this "blunder," rejected by Einstein, is still sometimes used by cosmologists even today, and the cosmological constant denoted by the Greek letter $\Lambda$ rears its ugly head again and again and again.

Friedmann wrote about his findings to Einstein, but did not get any answer. It happened that a theoretical physicist from Leningrad University, Professor Yuri Krutkov, had obtained permission to visit Berlin, which was not at all easy to accomplish in the early post-Revolutionary days in Russia. Friedmann asked Krutkov to try to see Einstein and to talk to him about it. As a result of his conversation, Einstein wrote Friedmann a short and somewhat grumpy letter, agreeing with his argument. Friedmann published his paper in 1922 in the German magazine *Zeitschrift für Physik,* thus opening a new era in cosmology.

In the same year the American astronomer Edwin Hubble of Mount Wilson Observatory proved that the so-called spiral nebulae are actually giant stellar galaxies floating in space far beyond the limits of the Milky Way, and the previously observed red shift of the lines in their spectra is to be interpreted as a result of their mutual recession. Further observational evidence provided indisputable proof of the theory of the expanding universe conceived theoretically by Friedmann. But he did not live to take part in the development of his brainchild. During one of his flights on a free meteorological balloon, Friedmann received a severe chill which resulted in pneumonia and death.

This ruined my plans to continue my work on relativistic cosmology, and I was "inherited" by Professor Krutkov, who suggested for my thesis the problem of "adiabatic invariance of a quantized pendulum with finite amplitudes." To put it very mildly, the project was extremely dull, and try as I might, I could not muster any enthusiasm for it.

The delay of one year, during which I did not have to attend any lectures or pass any examinations, caused me some trouble in my studies. The Commissariat of Education had just issued a decree adding two required courses to the curriculum in all faculties: one was "The History of World Revolution"; the other, "Dialectical Materialism."

Dialectical materialism is a branch of philosophy based

on principles developed in the nineteenth century by the
German philosopher G. W. F. Hegel. In spite of the fact
that I have passed an examination on that subject, I still
do not know what it is about and can only remember that
according to that way of thinking each argument must
consist of three parts: thesis, antithesis, and synthesis.
Marx, Engels, Lenin, and their followers used this philosophy to prove the correctness of Communistic sociology,
and it ultimately became the basic foundation of Com-
munism and played very much the same role as that of
Church dogma in the Middle Ages, sometimes assuming
grotesque forms. Everything had to conform to dialectical
materialism and any deviation from it was considered as
heresy and was severely punished. For me, dialectical materialism has only one great merit: it is subject to a *calem-
bour* which, unlike most puns, is adapted to almost per-
fect translation from Russian to other languages. In Russia the dirtiest way of swearing is based on wishing the opponent's mother all the worst things in the world. It is
known as *matershchina,* or maternal dialect. The *calem-
bour* is that, whereas the Soviet government always argues
by using dialectical materialism, the populace uses maternal dialect.

   Thus, I had to pass two examinations: one in the history of the world revolutionary movement and another in
the philosophy of dialectical materialism. The examinations were given, by the way, not by university professors
but by two men sent down from the Moscow Communistic Academy. The first examination was easy, because earlier I had read a great deal about the French Revolution
and the Paris Commune. When the examiner asked me
the date of the French Revolution, I quoted him a verse
reproduced here in English translation:

> A-hunting went the King in Vichy's woods that day.
> His dogs had tracked a deer, but then to his dismay

Came news of the revolt in Paris, an infernal
Disturbance to the hunt. Why and for what this *coup?*
The King lay down but, sleepless, noted in his journal
(Resentfully): "July Fourteenth: *Rien du tout!*"

The examiner was so much impressed by this verse that
he did not ask me what *year* the Revolution took place,
which of course I did not remember.

Much tougher was the examination in dialectical materialism, which did not make sense to me anyway. One of
the questions was "What is the difference between humans and animals?" Remembering my early religious education, I was almost ready to answer, "Humans have souls
while animals do not," which would have earned me a
complete failure. But I checked myself in time and said,
"None." "Wrong!" said the examiner; "according to this
book, humans use implements while animals do not." "I
am sorry," I responded. "As far as I know, monkeys throw
coconuts from trees at their enemies below, and if I am
not mistaken gorillas sometimes use big *dubinas* [thick
wooden sticks] in self-defense." I do not know whether or
not my statement was scientifically correct and leave it to
the zoology professors to arbitrate the dispute.

After I took these two examinations I was naturally
anxious to find out whether or not I had passed. Failure
would mean a whole year's delay in receiving the aspirantship. So I asked a Marxistically inclined student whom I
knew well to go to the examiner on dialectical materialism
and to ask him what my grade would be. Scratching his
head, the examiner said, "Gamow? Gamow, you say? Yes, I
remember, that was the gorilla with a stick. He was not
too bright, but I will pass him." This was the way I passed
satisfactorily my last two examinations.

But I am afraid that I begin to bore the reader with stories of my academic advances. There was, of course, another side of the picture, closely connected with the first.

This was the fellow students and the coeds. In 1924 there
arrived in Leningrad from Baku a peculiar character
named Lev Davidovich Landau [2] (Dau for short), followed by another newcomer from Poltava in the heart of
the Ukraine named Dmitri Dmitrievich Ivanienko
(Dimus, or Dim, for short). Both of them were highly interested in theoretical physics, and we formed a group
which was often jokingly called "the Three Musketeers."
This nucleus of young theoreticians was surrounded by a
group of satellites.

Dau and Dimus were a complete contrast to each other.
Dau was rather tall, very skinny, and, with his unruly
dark hair, resembled a broom turned upside down.
Dimus, on the other hand, could better have been com-
pared to a French brioche. As always happens, this group
of male students had an aureole of coeds, the most notable
being Irina (Ira) Sokolskaya, who was very talented in
drawing caricatures, and Yevgenia (Zhenya) Kanegiesser,[3]
who was extremely gifted in writing light verse.

Since theoreticians were not allotted private workrooms
(I lost mine when I said good-by to the interferometer),
our usual meeting place was the Borgman Library, which
grew from the donation of a large collection of books
willed to the Physics Institute by the late Professor Borgman. The library, occupying a couple of rooms lined with
bookshelves, was open to professors and aspirants and
served as the forum for the discussion of the problems of

[2] In 1962 Landau received the Nobel Prize for his outstanding work in
the field of low-temperature physics, eight months after he had been
pronounced clinically dead from injuries incurred in an automobile accident. An account of the dramatic medical techniques that saved his life
may be found in Alexander Dorozynski's *The Man They Wouldn't Let
Die* (New York: Macmillan, 1965).
[3] She eventually married a German theoretical physicist, Rudolf Peierls,
and left Russia, first for Germany and later (after Hitler came to power)
for England.

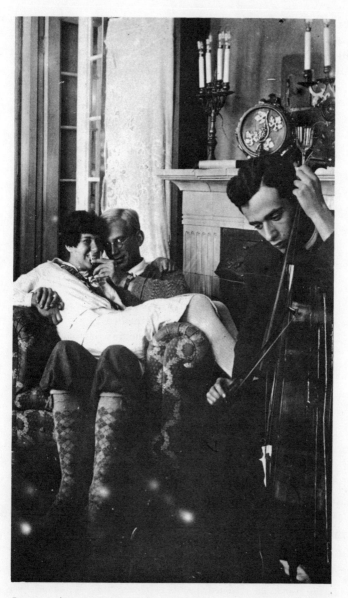

*In a private room at a restaurant: posed by George Gamow as the "guest," Yevgenia Kanegiesser as the "hostess," and Lev Landau as the "hired musician."*

modern physics and other matters. Here is an English version of a verse written by Zhenya about that cozy place:

> How snug the Bórgman athenaeum! [4]
> For more than five-and-twenty years
> Within this cheerful mausoleum
> Our theorists have met their peers.
>
> Here, famed for scientific talent,
>   Pillar of learning's *why* and *what*,
> Professor Bursián the gallant
>   Lolls in his clothes of foreign cut.
>
> And here, as the exam is looming,
>   Vladímir Alexándr'ich Fok,
> Mustache in shape from final grooming,
>   Composes questions round the clock.
>
> Here Ivaniénko listens, drowsing,
>   Sucker in mouth, to shimmy-beat.
> And Gámow, munching while he's browsing,
>   Eats all the choc'lates he can eat.
>
> To tuneful songs, Landáu the clever
>   Who'll gladly argue anywhere,
> At any time, with whomsoever,
>   Holds a discussion with a chair.

The rest of the time was occupied by playing tennis and by going swimming and to the movies, which showed Hollywood films [5] with Mary Pickford, Douglas Fairbanks, and other stars.

The years 1925 and 1926 brought much excitement into the field of theoretical physics. The famous quantum orbit model of the atom, formulated in 1913 by the Danish physicist Niels Bohr, which within one decade made

---

[4] In the names, the accented syllable is stressed. Please pronounce accordingly: Bur-si-án; Vla-dí-mir Al-ex-án-dr'ich; I-van-ién-ko; Gám-ov (broad *a*, of course, and *v* sound at end); Lan-dáu.

[5] There were, of course, also Russian films, but (in contrast to those produced later) they were awfully boring and nothing but propaganda.

tremendous advances in our understanding of the structure of the atom, ran into serious difficulties, and it became apparent that some radically new ideas were necessary to proceed with the development. Strangely enough, these ideas appeared simultaneously in two entirely different forms—so different that all theoretical physicists were completely puzzled. One was the so-called "matrix mechanics" proposed by a young German physicist, Werner Heisenberg; another was "wave mechanics," originally conceived by a Frenchman, Prince Louis de Broglie, and perfected by an Austrian, Erwin Schrödinger. It is impossible to explain in this book the principle of the two new atomic theories, and the only statement I can make is that they looked as different as a chicken fence and a pond. Nevertheless, both theories led to exactly the same results and explained equally well the observed properties of an atom on which Bohr's original theory ran on the rocks. But it was soon found that matrix and wave mechanics were physically identical and differed only in the "mathematical language" in which they were expressed. (Consider, for instance, the French and the German editions of the Bible, which look entirely different in print but are identical in content.) [6]

The new breakthrough in the theory of atomic and molecular structure resulted in hundreds of papers, and in our theoretical group at the University of Leningrad we spent all our time following the new publications and trying to understand them. All three of us (Dau, Dimus, and I) tried to use the new quantum theory for improving statistical physics but did not get anywhere.

In 1926 Dimus Ivanienko and I published a paper in

[6] A more detailed description of these theories on the popular level can be found in the author's books *Biography of Physics*, published by Harper in 1961, and *Thirty Years That Shook Physics*, published by Doubleday in 1966.

the German magazine *Zeitschrift für Physik*, in which we
attempted to consider the new quantity Ψ introduced by
Schrödinger as the fifth dimension, to be added to the relativistic four-dimensional world of Minkowski, which
consisted of three space coordinates with time as the
fourth. Later I learned that similar attempts had been
made by other physicists in Western Europe, but, although the idea looked very attractive, nothing good came
of it.

The next year I had a pleasant surprise when I opened
the new issue of *Zeitschrift für Physik*. It contained an article by W. Prokofiev and G. Gamow, on anomalous dis-
persion of light. I didn't even know that after I had
dropped this research Rogdestvenski gave it to another
student more skillful with his hands, who brought it to a
victorious conclusion. This was my first, and last, half-
paper on experimental physics.

During the first two years of my aspirantship I had
been trying to do some work on my official thesis on the
adiabatic invariants of a pendulum, but it was very difficult in view of the exciting new vistas opened by the ap-
pearance of wave mechanics, which superseded Bohr's
original quantum theory. In fact, if I had succeeded in my
task the results would soon have become of only historical
interest. I had made practically no progress during the
first year and still less during the second, and I had been
warned that if I did not show some reasonable progress
my aspirantship would not be extended for the third year.

At this point an unexpected change took place in my
career. An old, and at that time retired, professor, Orest
Danilovich Khvolson, from whom I had taken a freshman
course of physics (without attending a single lecture), suggested that I might get a boost by spending a few months
at a foreign university and said that he would be glad to
recommend to Leningrad University that I be sent for the

summer session of 1928 to the famous German university in Göttingen, one of the main centers in the development of quantum physics. At that time the main difficulty in visiting foreign countries was getting permission to exchange Russian rubles, which were not negotiable abroad, into the equivalent amount of foreign money (*valuta*) which could be used beyond the borders of the USSR. Khvolson's recommendation was cosigned by Krutkov and a few other professors who had a high opinion of my abilities, and early in June I stepped aboard a steamer sailing from Leningrad to the German port Swinemünde, to proceed from there by train to the city of Göttingen. Flocks of my friends came to the docks to see me off. There was a lot of shouting and handkerchief-waving, and Leningrad soon faded behind the grayish waters of the Gulf of Finland.

The arrival at Swinemünde was scheduled for early morning, and, awaiting the landing, I wrote to Zhenya, dating the postcard with a time unusual for me, 6:00 a.m. Next week the answer arrived:

> Greetings from you at six a. m.??
> They didn't seem the least surprising.
> Too overcome for poetizing,
> I simply shout "Hurrah!" pro tem.
>
> "Hurrah! Hurrah!" For now the fates
> In your direction are inclining.
> Planes! Cabs! Revues! (the silver lining!)
> Bananas! *Fräuleins!* Chocolates!
>
> You didn't change your milk-white slacks? [7]
> You're hopeless, Geo.! . . . Dau raved and ranted
> Because his passport wasn't granted,
> And cast about for rope or ax.

[7] Because of the shortage of clothes in Russia at that time, the only decent-looking pair of trousers I had to wear on the trip were white tennis pants.

But now he yields to his defeat
(And boils with inner irritation!)
He'll sail the Vólga on vacation,
Play tennis till the August heat.

Dimus seeks fame the Alpine way,
Hoards hobnails in his new bandanna.
Poltáva-bound, he and Oksána
Took off—God bless them!—yesterday.

Mercury arcs illuminate
My photographic coffin. In it
I'm snapping spectra every minute.
I like my job; it's really great.

It rains all summer—rain, rain, rain!
You lucky boy, your lot I covet;
Still, for Odessa (how I love it!)
I'll soon be leaving on the train.

From Gretchens what can you expect?
And so, hands off the *Fräuleins* (misses)!
To Fok and you I genuflect
And send—by mail, of course—some kisses.

I hope this letter makes you glad.
Farewell, dear Geo., my *bon ami!*
Nina [8] says: "Write!" and so does

**Z.**

Fourteenth of June        . . . in Leningrad.

[8] Nina is the name of Zhenya's sister.

# 3

## Abroad in Göttingen, Copenhagen, and Cambridge

I arrived in Göttingen in the late afternoon and, after checking my suitcase at the station, went to see the only man I knew in the city, Vladimir Fok, who was an assistant professor at Leningrad University. He had also managed to get permission from the Soviet government to attend summer school abroad, but had arrived in Göttingen a few days earlier than I. I found him ready to go to a party which Professor Max Born, the Director of the Institute of Theoretical Physics at the university, was giving for his staff and senior students at a restaurant on Nikolausberg.

"Come along," said Fok, "I am sure Professor Born will be glad to see you." So I went to what turned out to be a typical German party, with dancing and such games as using soup spoons to pick up potatoes arranged on the floor or attempting to capture, with one's teeth alone, apples floating in a bucket. There was also a reasonable amount of Münchner beer, and a divine liqueur called Kloster Geist.

Speaking of Professor Born, I must inject here a story of something that happened a few years later. Because of the increasing pressure of Nazism, Born was forced to emigrate and accepted an invitation to Cambridge University. When he came out of the railway station in Cambridge he saw a giant poster saying:

BORN TO BE HANGED

This was a shock! He had seen many similar posters in Nazi Germany, referring to various anti-Nazis. But here, in free England, to see such a statement, and concerning himself at that, was unbelievable. However, the Cambridge people who met him at the station quieted him quickly by explaining that this was only an advertisement for a play to be presented in the local theater and that "born" was just the past tense of the verb "to be born."

Professor Born's Nikolausberg party lasted until rather late at night, and then everybody went home carrying Chinese lanterns on sticks. I escorted a young coed whose English was as bad as my German, but somehow we understood each other. Arriving at the house in which she lived, she said gently, "Good *nacht!*" to which I answered "*Gut* night!" and was left alone on the street.

While taking her home I had completely lost my sense of direction, which is quite excusable because I had never been in this city before. So I went straight ahead until I ran into a not very tall earth dam. About this structure I had heard before. It was the *Wahlenpromenade,* the remnants of the medieval wall surrounding the city, and I knew if I crossed it I would be out in the country.

So I turned back and finally reached the central part of Göttingen. It was dark except for a few street lanterns, and there was nobody on the streets to ask for directions. Then just by chance I saw a building with the sign HOTEL ZUM KRONPRINZEN. The building was completely dark and the doors were tightly locked. Nevertheless, I pulled the bell handle vigorously several times, and finally the sleepy

porter opened the door. He informed me that there was a
*Korporantensammlung* in the city and that all hotels were
completely full. Giving him a coin for his trouble, I decided to walk the streets all night until the city woke up
again. Suddenly I heard the sound of music coming from
somewhere and, turning the corner, saw an illuminated
tavern (I think it was *Die Drei Rosen,* although I am not
sure) filled with people. When I entered, a spherical, sym-
metrical hostess rushed to me, carrying three beer steins
in each hand, and asked, *"Was möchten Sie haben, mein
Herr?"*

*"Ich will Zimmer zu schlafen,"* said I in my poor German.

*"Oh, ja! Natürlich!"* said she, and explained that she
had a room with a big bed upstairs. She escorted me up,
with a candlestick in her hand, and, noticing that I had
no luggage (the station's checking counter closed very
early), asked to be paid in advance. I paid the required
amount and wished her good night. A few minutes later,
before I had managed even to undress, she knocked on
the door again and brought in two towels which were
originally absent from the room.

*"Vielen Dank,"* said I. *"Gut nacht!"*

She looked at me suspiciously and asked if I was alone.
*"Ja, liebe Frau, ich bin allein,"* said I, dying to go to
sleep.

*"Aber, junger Mann!"* she exclaimed, and explained
that if I would go downstairs I could easily find many
beautiful *Mädchen.*

*"Oh, nein!"* said I. *"Ich will schlafen.* Good *nacht!"*
And I collapsed into the bed.

The next morning, after a good dish of *Spiegel Eier
und Schinken,* I walked out of this exciting establishment
and found a more quiet place to live. It was a *Moblierte*

*Zimmer zu vermieten* [1] (furnished room for rent) belonging to the widow of a university professor. She placed me
in her late husband's study, with walls lined with bookshelves, a huge mahogany desk, and a large leather sofa,
which could be turned into a bed at night.

Göttingen is a charming little city with an old and famous university. At that time, in the field of theoretical
physics it could compete even with Copenhagen. It was
buzzing with excitement caused by wave and matrix mechanics, which had been developed only two years before
my arrival there. Both seminar rooms and cafés were
crowded with physicists, old and young, arguing about the
consequences which this new development in the quantum theory would have in our understanding of atomic
and molecular structure. But somehow I was not engulfed
in this whirlpool of feverish activity. One reason was that
far too many people were involved in it, whereas I always
preferred to work in less crowded fields. Another reason
was that whereas any new theory is almost always expressed originally in very simple form, within only a few
years it usually grows into an extremely complicated
mathematical structure requiring oodles and oodles of
"exing" (*Exerei,* as Einstein used to call it, deriving the
name from the letter x used as an unknown quantity in
calculations). When I was a young student in Odessa I
planned to become a mathematician, and for me "real"
pure mathematics included such fields as the theory of
numbers, topology, and the theory of infinite sets (*Men-
genlehre*). But the so-called calculus, extending into ordinary, partial, and integro-differential equations never had
any appeal for me, and I was always losing my way in it.
Of course I knew that it is absolutely necessary for the sol-

[1] Whenever I hear or pronounce these words it always reminds me of
Heinrich Heine. I read somewhere that the rhythm of Heine's verses is
identical with the rhythm in this phrase.

ution of complicated scientific and engineering problems, but I just did not like it.

Thus, while all the quantum physicists in the world were attacking atoms and molecules, I decided to see what the new quantum theory could do in the case of the atomic nucleus. To start with, I went to the university library to look through the recent literature on experimental nuclear physics. The very first day I ran into an article by Ernest Rutherford in *Philosophical Magazine* (volume 4, page 580, 1927), in which he describes an experiment on the scattering of alpha particles in uranium. Using very fast alpha particles emitted by the polonium isotope RaC', he found no deviations from his famous scattering formula. This indicated that the Coulomb repulsive forces which oppose the penetration of alpha particles into the nucleus hold down to the distance of at least $3.2 \times 10^{-12}$ cm from the center of the nucleus. This finding stood in direct contradiction to the fact that uranium, being a radioactive element itself, emits alpha particles with energy about half that of the RaC''s alpha particles. How could this be? The fact that alpha particles remain in the uranium nucleus for a long time indicates that Coulomb repulsion turns into attraction at some distance smaller than $3.2 \times 10^{-12}$ cm (for uranium), thus forming a potential barrier which prevents the bombarding alpha particles from getting into the nucleus, and also prohibits those which are inside from getting out. How could it be that bombarding high-energy particles cannot get over the barrier from outside, while at the same time internal alpha particles, which have only one-half as much energy, manage to leak out, even though sometimes rather slowly? To explain this paradoxical situation, Rutherford proposed in his article a hypothesis that, starting from the nucleus, each alpha particle carries along two electrons which neu-

tralize its positive charge and make the Coulomb force in-
effective. When this neutralized alpha particle is well beyond the rim of the barrier, the electrons separate from it
and return into the nucleus, as two tugs would leave a
large ocean liner which they have just pulled out of the
harbor. This explanation did not appeal to me at all, and
before I closed the magazine I knew what actually happens in this case. It was a typical phenomenon which
would be impossible in classical Newtonian mechanics,
but was in fact to be expected in the case of the new wave
mechanics. In wave mechanics there are no impenetrable
barriers, and, as the British physicist R. H. Fowler put it
after my lecture on that subject at the Royal Society of
London the same winter, "Anyone present in this room
has a finite chance of leaving it without opening the door,
or, of course, without being thrown out through the window."

The motion of material particles is governed by the so-
called "pilot-waves," first proposed by Louis de Broglie.
These waves, propagating freely through space where material particles can also move without any difficulty,
"leak" slowly through the regions into which, according to
Newtonian mechanics, these particles cannot penetrate at
all. And if the de Broglie wave gets through, even though
with some difficulty, it always smuggles a particle with it.

Having returned to my room from the library, I took
pencil and paper and wrote a simple formula for the probability of such wave-mechanical penetration. But a difficulty arose. To evaluate this formula I had to calculate
the integral of the expression $\sqrt{1 - \dfrac{a}{r}}\, dr$, and I did not
know how to do it. So I went to see my friend N. Kot-
shchin, a Russian mathematician who was also spending
that summer in Göttingen. He didn't believe me when I
said that I could not take that integral, saying that he
would give a failing grade to any student who couldn't do

such an elementary task. When I wrote the paper for publication, I expressed at the end of it my thanks to Kotshchin for his help with mathematics. Later, when the paper appeared, he wrote me that he had become a laughingstock among his colleagues, who had learned what kind of highbrow mathematical help he had given me.

The theory of the potential barrier not only removed Rutherford's paradoxical result with alpha bombardment of uranium, but also explained the well-known mysterious empirical relation between the energies of alpha particles emitted by different radioactive substances and their mean periods of half-life, known as the Geiger-Nuttall law, which was first formulated by Geiger and Nuttall in 1911. They noticed that the higher is the energy of the emitted alpha particles, the shorter is the life of the radioactive substance emitting them. Plotting in logarithmic scale the mean lifetimes of various radioactive elements against their alpha-particle energies, they obtained an almost straight line running from uranium with an alpha-particle energy of only 4.1 Mev (million electron volts) and a mean half-life of 4.5 billion years, all the way down to RaC′ with an alpha-particle energy of 7.7 Mev and a mean half-life of only 0.0002 seconds. The curve which I calculated on the basis of the wave-mechanical theory runs right smack through the experimental points.

With the ever-accelerated rate of scientific research and the rapidly increasing number of people pursuing it, it happens more and more often that important discoveries are made simultaneously and independently by two or more people, or several groups of people. This was the case with my theory of radioactive alpha decay, which was conceived at the same time by Ronald Gurney in collaboration with Edward Condon. In fact, their paper, which was published in *Nature,* was received by the editors several days earlier than my paper, which was published in

*Zeitschrift für Physik.* Such coincidences of important discoveries result in the gradual dilution of the annual Nobel Prizes (neither Gurney and Condon nor I received one or a fraction thereof), and in the near future a successful scientist may be able to say, "I got three-seventeenths of the Nobel Prize for 19———."

During my stay in Göttingen I made friends with a jolly Austrian-born physicist, Fritz Houtermans. He had recently completed his Ph.D. in experimental physics but was always quite enthusiastic about theoretical problems. When I told him about my work on the theory of alpha decay, he insisted that it must be done with higher precision and in more detail. Being a native Viennese, he could work only in a café, and I will always remember him sitting with a slide rule at a table covered with papers and a dozen or so empty coffee cups. (During that period, when one asked for more coffee in Germany, the waiter always brought a new cup, leaving the empty ones on the table to be counted in making up the bill.) We also tried to use the old electric (not electronic, of course) computer in the university's Mathematical Institute, but it always went haywire after midnight. We ascribed this interference to the ghost of Karl Friedrich Gauss arriving to inspect his old place.

But the summer semester was coming to an end; Fritz was to move to Berlin, and I had to return to Leningrad. However, on my way back I wanted to stop for a day in Copenhagen and, if possible, to meet the almost mythical Niels Bohr, for whom I had great admiration.

Thus I arrived in Copenhagen (spelled København), where ø is the characteristic Danish guttural o. They say that the best way to learn to pronounce it is to listen to the honking of the taxis in that city. According to the theory advanced by the Czechoslovakian physicist George

Placzek, many Danes are so fat because they swallow air pronouncing ø. This letter is most often encountered in the word *øre*, the Danish monetary unit. Since my money was practically all gone, I stopped in a cheap rooming house and walked to the Institute for Theoretical Physics on Blegdamsvej. Bohr's secretary, Frøken Betty Schultz, who served in the institute for half a century, from its foundation in 1918 until her retirement in January 1968, said that the professor was very busy and that I might have to wait for a few days. However, when I told her that

*Niels Henrick David Bohr.* Left: *At the age of 25 (photograph by his then future mother-in-law).* Right: *At the age of 76 (photograph by the author).*

I had just enough money left to stay for one day before
leaving for home, the interview was arranged for the same
afternoon.

Bohr asked me what I was doing at present, and I told
him about the quantum theory of radioactive alpha decay;
my paper was in the press but had not yet appeared. Bohr
listened with interest and then said, "My secretary told
me that you have only enough money to stay here for a
day. If I arrange for you a Carlsberg Fellowship at the
Royal Danish Academy of Sciences,[2] would you stay here
for one year?"

"My, yes, thank you!" I answered very enthusiastically.

Carlsberg is the best beer in the world, or at least all
people who have ever worked with Bohr think so. When
the old fellow Carlsberg died, he willed the income from
the brewery to the Royal Danish Academy of Sciences and
made a provision that his palatial mansion, located right
in the middle of the brewery (with fermentation tanks
hidden by the surrounding trees), was to be occupied by
the most famous Danish scientist.

When I first came to Copenhagen, the house was occupied by Knud Rasmussen, the explorer of Greenland.
After Rasmussen's death, Niels Bohr moved in, and today
the house is occupied by the renowned Danish astronomer
Bengt Strømgren. The most impressive part of the house
is probably the dining room, one wall of which is made of
glass and separates the dining area from the greenhouse
with decorative plants and singing birds.

It is typical that the brewery's "research and development" laboratory was run by the well-known biochemist
Lindestrøm Lang. When he celebrated his sixtieth birthday a special necktie was produced in a limited edition in
his honor. This tie showed a bottle of Carlsberg Pilsner. I

[2] Of which I have had the honor to be a foreign member since 1951.

got one from Lindestrøm Lang in exchange for an RNA tie, which is discussed on page 147.

Yes, old man Carlsberg did a good deed, and it is a pity that in the United States there are no Schlitz or Ballantine fellowships distributed by the National Academy of Sciences.

As soon as it was decided that I would stay with Bohr, Frøken Schultz found me a nice *pension* to live in on Triangular Square, a few blocks from the institute. "We have not had experience with this place before," she told me, "but they say it is good."

Thus I moved the very same day to this *pension* run by Frøken Have and did not even sleep in the rooming house's bed, for which I had to pay a few *kroner* in advance. Frøken Have's *pension* turned out indeed to be an excellent place, and many physicists who came to Copenhagen later stayed there. Bohr himself used to drop in once in a while, and the proud Frøken Have considered her place as an "annex" to his institute.

The work in Bohr's institute was completely free; one could come in the morning as late as one wanted (usually very late), and stay as long as one wanted at night, playing Ping-pong and discussing physics and what not. However, there was always one exception: the man who served as Bohr's assistant in research would have to be bound by Bohr's own schedule. Bohr could not think unless he was talking to somebody, and also did not want to do any mathematics. The generations of Bohr's "co-talkers" (though he usually did all the talking) included such persons as Hendrick Kramers (Netherlands), Oscar Klein (Sweden), George Placzek (Czechoslovakia), and Leon Rosenfeld (Belgium), who remained with Bohr until his death. I was never in danger of being drafted for that job because Bohr knew very well that I was even worse than he in complicated mathematical computations and would

*The coat of arms for Bohr's Institute created by the author in 1929.*

be of no help in the phraseology and grammar of a foreign language. But, along with great honor, this position demanded all-day, and often late-evening, work.

Being left to my own devices, I continued to work on the theory of the nuclear potential barrier, reversing the case of spontaneous alpha decay and calculating the probability of alpha particles bombarding the nucleus from outside to penetrate into the nuclear interior. The results of my calculations were in very good agreement with Rutherford's experiments in which he managed to crack atomic nuclei of light elements by hitting them with fast alpha particles.

Bohr wanted me to go to England to show my calculations to Rutherford, but he told me that I must be very careful in presenting the quantum theory of nuclear transformation to him, since the old man did not like any innovations and used to say that any theory is good only if it is simple enough to be understood by a barmaid. The difficulty was that, as I have explained before, at the end of his paper on the penetration of RaC' alpha particles into the nuclei of uranium atoms which prompted my work on the potential barrier penetration, Rutherford proposed a classical explanation of that paradoxical phenomenon based on the idea that the alpha particles come part of the way out of the Coulomb field of the nucleus carrying no electric charge. For many years before the discovery of neutrons, Rutherford had been a believer in the existence of the chargeless proton, or neutron, and an intensive hunt for it was carried out in the Cavendish Laboratory. However, in spite of all his experimental genius and the help of gifted young physicists like James Chadwick, the neutron stubbornly refused to be detected until its existence was finally proved by Chadwick in 1932 on the basis of the series of experiments started in Germany by W. Bothe and continued in France by Frédéric and Irène Joliot-Curie. To explain the decay of uranium along classical lines, Rutherford imagined that an alpha particle during the early stages of its emission consists of four neutral protons (a polyneutron, as one would say now) and thus is not influenced by the electric charge of the nucleus. As I mentioned earlier, Rutherford believed that at a certain distance from the nuclear surface the two electrons accompanying the alpha particle, like two tugs pulling a large ship out of a narrow harbor, become disengaged and return to port, while the ship continues to speed up on its own power. This certainly was a brilliant idea, which, however, was unfortunately disposed of by the newborn wave mechanics.

Well, Bohr was afraid that the same thing might happen to me with Rutherford as happened to him (Bohr) when, sixteen years earlier, he went to Cambridge to work

*Sir J. J. Thomson and Sir Ernest Rutherford (later Baron Rutherford of Nelson) in the courtyard of Cavendish Laboratory after a meeting.*

with J. J. Thomson and dared to disagree with Thomson's pet theory of the internal structure of an atom. Thus, Bohr had written a long diplomatic letter to Rutherford about me (I never saw the letter), and I carried with me to England a Christmas present for Rutherford which, both Bohr and I hoped, would save me from the powerful jaws of the Crocodile.[3] The strategic present

[3] Rutherford was nicknamed the Crocodile by one of his favorite students, Peter Kapitza. In Russian fairy tales the crocodile is not considered a vicious reptile but represents a symbol of robust power. In fact, on the wall of the special laboratory which Rutherford built for Kapitza's research is a bas-relief of a life-sized crocodile, the meaning of which was never officially explained.

consisted of two neatly plotted sets of points representing Rutherford's latest experiments on the artificial transformations of light nuclei bombarded by alpha particles of different radioactive elements. One set of points showed that, for a given kind of bombarded nuclei, the yield of protons rapidly increased with the energy of the bombarding particles. The second graph showed that, for a given energy of alpha projectiles, the yield of protons rapidly decreased with the atomic number of the bombarded elements, becoming indistinguishable from zero beyond aluminum. Through the experimental points run two theoretical curves, a rising and a descending one, calculated by me during my first few months in Copenhagen on the basis of the wave-mechanical theory of the penetration of a plain alpha wave through the potential barrier surrounding the nuclei of light elements.

Since even Rutherford would oppose the idea of two tugs going too far out in the water to meet the ship and bring it to dock, the stratagem worked, and I was accepted into the Cavendish family.

Upon my return from England I received a letter from Fritz Houtermans, who was now at the University of Berlin. He wrote that, together with a visiting British astronomer, Robert Atkinson, he had arrived at a very interesting idea concerning the possibility of nuclear-energy liberation in the sun and other stars. Atkinson knew all about the recent work of Sir Arthur Eddington which made it possible to calculate the temperatures and densities in the central regions of stars, and was wondering whether the violent thermal collisions between the atomic nuclei could produce enough energy to account for the radiation from their surfaces. My paper on the wave-mechanical theory of artificial transformations of light elements had not yet been published, but of course Fritz knew all about it from our correspondence. They decided that by using my formula one could calculate purely theoretically the rates of thermonuclear reactions, as we named them, in the stellar interior.

Since Robert was an observational astronomer and Fritz an experimental physicist, I had to help them with the theoretical part of the program. We decided that the best place to discuss things was some skiing resort in the Alps, and in the early spring I got on a train and, after picking up Fritz and Robert on the way in Berlin, proceeded with them to a small skiing hotel called Alpenrose (of course!) in Zürs Vorarlberg, a village in the Austrian Alps. They were almost ready with their calculations, so the discussion did not impose on our skiing time. All they wanted to ask me concerned some details which they did not know how to handle. The main problem was to find out what happens to a proton when it penetrates into the nucleus of a light element. It would not have enough energy to eject an alpha particle, and besides, its penetration would introduce a second potential barrier for the outgoing particle. Thus it seemed most likely that the proton would be captured through the emission of the excess energy in the form of a gamma ray. What would be the probability of such an emission? It must be remembered that in 1929 neutrons had not yet been discovered, and the nucleus was thought to be built of protons and electrons, although even at that time there were serious difficulties in accepting electrons as independent constituent parts of nuclear structure. So when they asked me about the probability of gamma emission, I advised them to use J. J. Thomson's theoretical formula for dipole radiation. It must be remembered that there are many different types of electric fields between charges. One is the dipole field between two opposite charges, which results in their mutual attraction. Another is the quadrupole field between the two charges of the same sign, which results in mutual repulsion. There are also the octopole and higher *n*-pole fields formed by a larger number of positive and negative charges that result in more complicated interactions.

When the charges oscillate, the field surrounding them propagates in all different directions, forming electromagnetic waves and carrying away energy. In the case of the dipole emitter the intensity of radiation is the largest; it is much smaller for the quadrupole, and decreases rapidly for the *n*-poles of higher order. If atomic nuclei consisted of particles of opposite charge (as the atom itself does), the gamma-ray emission would be very strong. If, as we now know, the nucleus is built of protons and neutrons which carry no electric charge, the field surrounding them is more similar to a quadrupole and the intensity should be calculated by using the quadrupole formula. Now, the emission intensity of a quadrupole is reduced in respect to that of a dipole by a factor $\left( \dfrac{\text{size of the emitter}}{\text{emitted wave length}} \right)^2$ which in the case of gamma rays emitted by atomic nuclei is 1/10,000. Thus, taking my advice, Atkinson and Houtermans overestimated the probability of radioactive capture of a proton by a factor of ten thousand. My only consolation for giving this wrong advice is that the fact that the emission of a gamma ray is governed by the quadrupole and not the dipole formula was proved two years later (still before the discovery of neutrons) by another student of Bohr named Max Delbrück and myself. We did this by comparing the probability of gamma-ray emission with that of the ejection of the so-called long-range alpha particles.

But there was still another mistake made in the Atkinson-Houtermans calculations which was also due to the state of nuclear physics in that early era. Following my paper on the theory of Rutherford's experiment on the artificial disintegration of elements, they assumed that the probability of a bombarding proton's striking a nucleus, called the collision cross section, was of the order of magnitude of the geometrical nuclear cross section. Instead, as was learned later, they should have taken the square of the de Broglie wave of the incident protons. In my theory of Rutherford's experiments this really did not make any difference, since the bombarding alpha particles came from radioactive nuclei and hence their de Broglie wave lengths were naturally of the same order of magnitude as the nuclear diameters (i.e., about $10^{-12}$ cm).

However, in the case of thermal protons at the intrasolar temperature of 20 million degrees, the de Broglie wave length is a hundred times larger than the nuclear diameter and, taking the square of the latter instead of the square of the former, one underestimates the probability of a collision by a factor of ten thousand. Fortunately the error introduced by using the dipole formula counteracted this mistake, since $\frac{10,000}{10,000} = 1$, so that the figures for the rate of energy production in the solar interior as given in the original paper of Houtermans and Atkinson were essentially correct. This mix-up probably represents one of the most striking examples in the history of science of a case in which rapid advance can suffer from the pitfalls of nonconsolidated, by-passed ground. In fact, the correct formula for the rate of the thermonuclear reaction, which uses the correct collision cross section and the quadrupole emission formula, was not published until six or seven years later by Edward Teller and myself.

In their paper on thermonuclear reactions, Houtermans and Atkinson concluded that the only reactions suitable for explaining energy production in the sun are those between the protons and the nuclei of some light element

between lithium and neon in the periodic table. It was
years before the construction of artificial accelerators permitted the study of nuclear reactions caused by proton impacts, and the only information available was based on alpha-particle bombardment. However, Houtermans and
Atkinson suggested that the process was a cyclic one in
which four protons are captured consecutively by a nucleus and then are ejected in the form of an alpha particle. In fact the tentative title of their paper was: *"Wie
kann man ein Helium Kern in einen potential Topf kö-
chen?"* ("How can one cook a helium nucleus in a potential pot?") This was changed to a more trivial title by the
unimaginative editor of *Zeitschrift für Physik*. And not
until ten years after the publication of Houtermans' and
Atkinson's paper was enough experimental evidence accumulated concerning nuclear reactions, particularly in the
processes involving proton impacts, to permit us to disen-
tangle the details of thermonuclear reactions in stars. This
led to the well-known carbon cycle, proposed independently in 1938 by Carl von Weizsäcker in Germany and
Hans Bethe in the United States, and the reaction between two colliding protons studied by Charles Critchfield and Bethe.

In the spring of 1929 I was facing the problem of what
to do in the summer. My Carlsberg fellowship, which was
actually for only ten months, was coming to an end. I was
sure that I would get a Rockefeller fellowship for spending a year in Cambridge, for which I had applied at Rutherford's and Bohr's suggestion, but it would not start until
the fall. On the other hand, my stipend for the third year
of aspirantship in Leningrad University had been accumulating there through the winter, and more was due for
the summer months. Thus the logical conclusion was to

spend that summer in Russia, and that was what I did.
In Russia I encountered a warm and jubilant reception.
The newspapers proclaimed:

> A son of the working class [*ot stanka* [4]] has explained the
> tiniest piece of machinery in the world: the nucleus of an
> atom.

> A Soviet fellow has shown the West that Russian soil can
> produce her own Platos and sharp-witted Newtons.[5]

*Pravda,* the official organ of the Communist Party, carried on the first page a verse by Demian Biedny: [6]

> The USSR has been labeled the land of the yokel and
>    Khamov.[7]
> Quite right! And we have an example in this Soviet fel-
>    low named Gamow.
> Why, this working-class bumpkin, this dimwit, this
>    Gyorgy Anton'ich called Geo.,
> He went and caught up with the atom and kicked it
>    about like a pro.

> On the point of a needle, they tell us, are trillions of
>    atoms and more.
> But *he* pounced upon *one single atom* and straight to the
>    nucleus bore,
> And he then was so all-fired clever, so goldarned ingen-
>    ious and deft,
> That Crack! Crack! Crack! Crack! went the victim, till
>    only the fragments were left.

[4] *Stanok* in Russian means "lathe."
[5] Based on a quotation from the eighteenth-century Russian poet and scientist Mikhail Lomonosov.
[6] A Soviet government verse-writer, strongly disliked by all Russian poets,
who wrote on various political and social problems in a simple peasant
style similar to that of the fable-writer Krylov of the early nineteenth century.
[7] My name, Gamow, rhymes with "Khamov," which is the genitive case of
Kham (Ham). Kham, the second son of Noah (Shem, Ham, and Japheth), is
a symbol for an uncultivated person.

So the Riddle of Riddles was solved by our poor little
   commonplace nation!
What on earth can this possibly mean? Does it herald a
   slight variation
In long-held illusions about us? Do we now measure up
   to the rest?
This Gamow is surely a caution. (Take warning, ye lands
   of the West!)

Variation or no variation, the message is graphic and
   sober:
In science right now there arises the potent bouquet of
   October.

Ironically, this verse about me was followed by a second
verse by Biedny on another scientific topic: a discovery by
a scientist from GIMZ (State Institute of Medical Knowledge) of an ointment for curing a black eye, instead of the
conventional beefsteaks, which were hard to get.

After arriving in Leningrad from Copenhagen, I went
first to Odessa to visit my aging father, and from there for
a few weeks' stay at the Simeis Astronomical Observatory
in the Crimea, where I had some friends. The rest of the
summer I spent on the beach not far from Yalta. The only
amusing thing that happened that summer was connected
with a medical examination. I received from the Paris office of the Rockefeller Foundation a thick envelope containing various questionnaires which had to be filled out
by applicants for fellowships. Among them was a questionnaire concerning my physical condition. The fellowship
committee apparently wanted to be sure that the candidate was healthy enough not to die soon after receiving
the grant spent on him, in which case the money would
evidently go to waste. There must have been some physi-
cians in Yalta, but I was afraid that none of them knew
enough English to fill out the questionnaire. Fortunately,

I knew a young woman doctor from Moscow who was also vacationing on my beach. She had spent one year attending the university in Edinburgh, Scotland, and knew English better than I did at that time. Unfortunately she was an ophthalmologist (something to do with the eyes) and also had not brought her black bag with her. But she happened to carry along a book on general medicine from which she could pick up the normal figures for such clinical findings as the blood pressure and sugar content in the urine. She told me to jump on one foot while she filled out the questionnaire from the book, and I apparently stand as the most normal person on the medical records of the foundation. Also I did not die soon thereafter, so no harm was done.

But this is not the end of the story. Returning to Leningrad, I found a disquieting letter from the Rockefeller Foundation saying that I must have a serious heart disease. In fact, the blood pressure during the contraction of my heart was lower than during the expansion, a sympton indicating an extreme sclerosis. Fortunately I knew the Moscow address of my woman doctor, and on my request she informed the foundation that just by a mistake she had reversed the two figures on the blood-pressure chart. Thus the fellowship was granted, and at the end of September I departed for England, after obtaining a passport from Narkompros (the People's Commissariat of Education), to work with Rutherford for a year at the Cavendish Laboratory of Cambridge University.

When I arrived at Cambridge I felt as if I were coming home to an old familar place. I took lodgings in a typical student complex in Victoria Park, with a study downstairs, a bedroom upstairs, and an amicable old widow, Mrs. Webb, in the background. I opened a bank account to deposit my monthly Rockefeller paychecks. I bought myself a pair of plus fours for golfing, an art which I never mastered in spite of all the instruction from my good friend John Cockcroft. I also bought a second-hand BSA (Birmingham Small Arms) motorcycle to get back and forth from the Cavendish Laboratory and to drive around the countryside. In such circumstances life was composed of a sequence of events—highly exciting events, medium-exciting events, and other, not especially exciting, events. Thus I will go on, event by event.

The first was undoubtedly the visit of Nevil Francis Mott, my old friend from Copenhagen days. He came in excitedly, exclaiming, "Gamow! How did you manage to get this house?"

"What is so particular about it?" I asked.

"Come out and see."

So I did, and he pointed to the name of the house, over the entrance. It read: KREMLIN. Well, this was a "coincidental event."

Another event, also connected with Russia, took place when, coming to Cavendish one day, I was told that Rutherford was urgently looking for me. I hurried to his office and found him sitting at his desk with a letter in his hand. "What the hell do they mean?" he shouted, pushing the letter at me. The letter, handwritten on rather cheap stationery, read something like this:

> 10 October 1929
> Rostow na Donu
> USSR

Dear Professor Rutherford,
    We students of our university physics club elect you our honorary president because you proved that atoms have balls.

> Secretary:
> Kondrashenko

Well, it took me some time to explain this to him. The point is that what in English is called the atomic nucleus, and in German *Atom Kern* (atom stone, as in a fruit), is called in Russian *atomnoie iadro,* the latter word being the same as in cannonball. Thus, in consulting a bilingual dictionary, the Russian students picked up the wrong term. After Rutherford had stopped roaring with laughter, which brought half the laboratory to his door, he called his secretary and dictated a very nice letter to the students' club, thanking them for the honor.

Another occasion upon which I was called to Rutherford's office had some more significant scientific consequences. He had in front of him a current issue of *Zeitschrift für Physik* with an article by H. Pose from Halle am Saale. Pose was studying protons emitted from an aluminum filament under the action of alpha-particle bombardment. As a rule in such experiments one uses very thin metal foils so that an alpha particle passing through them does not have a chance to lose much of its initial energy. Thus the protons knocked from the atomic nuclei all have the same energy and show a sharply defined range in the air behind the foil. In this particular set of experiments, however, Pose used aluminum foils which were thick enough to stop completely all alpha particles entering them, so that only protons were emerging from the other side. This was done for convenience, since with such an arrangement one would not have to worry about mistaking an alpha particle for a proton. What Rutherford objected to was the fact that the protons observed by Pose represented a homogeneous group. Indeed, since the particles passing the foil would have energy continuously decreasing with the depth of their penetration into the metal, one would expect that the ejected protons would also have a continuous energy distribution. But the curves shown in Pose's paper indicated sharply defined energies, and Rutherford was completely right in saying, "This fellow measured something wrong."

At that point an idea occurred to me. A few days before, I had read in *Nature* a letter to the editors written by Ronald Gurney, whose name I have mentioned earlier in connection with the quantum theory of alpha decay. In that letter Gurney suggested that if the motion of alpha particles is governed by de Broglie waves, one should expect associated resonance phenomena in their collision with the nuclei when their energies were just right. In the case of Pose's thick foils, the resonance could take place in some sharply defined layer in the middle of the foil, in which case the energy of the ejected protons would also be sharply defined.

Thus Rutherford wrote to Pose, suggesting to him a "sliced sausage" experiment. In that experiment Pose sliced his aluminum foil in about a dozen layers. Actually, he did not slice it, but rather substituted for it a "layer cake" of about a dozen foils, each of them being correspondingly thinner. In order to fool the alpha particles, one of these subfoils was made not of aluminum but of copper, the thickness of which was such as to result in exactly the same stopping power as the aluminum foil. Placing his foil pack into the beam of alpha particles, Pose started "listing" it—that is, moving aluminum subfoils from the front to the rear end so that the "fake aluminum," or copper, foil occupied alternatively different positions in the interior of the layer cake. Protons continued to emerge with the usual strength until after one move they suddenly disappeared. One more move, and they were back again. The situation was clear: at this particular position of the copper foil the protons entered it with somewhat higher energy than the resonance value for aluminum and exited with energy lower than necessary to produce the resonance in the subsequent aluminum foils.

This description today of Pose's experiment appears to
be rather boring, but at the time it was carried out the
results were very exciting, as it demonstrated a typical
wave phenomenon, giving additional confirmation to the
new ideas about matter and its motion. And, of course,
the discovery of the nuclear resonance opened new vistas
for future studies of the structure of matter.

Now may be as good a time as any to tell about another
Cambridge event—or rather a phenomenon—known
as Peter Kapitza. He came to Cambridge from Leningrad
in the early twenties as an unknown young physicist and
experienced an unprecedented rise to glory. His uncanny
gift for building ingenious gadgets soon attracted the attention of Rutherford, who also liked to indulge in this
art. And in physics, in those days at least, to have a little
gadget could mean having a nucleus for sixpence. True
enough, Kapitza's gadget began to grow larger and larger,
and it finally developed into a machine with a giant, massive flywheel for storing mechanical energy to be released
for a negligible fraction of a second into a small wire coil,
which then exploded with a loud bang. But just before
that coil exploded it produced in its interior the strongest
magnetic field that could be produced in the world at that
time. And quickly, quickly, Kapitza measured the effect of
that field on the different elements in Mendeleev's periodic table. He kept all the elements he used in his experiments in a cupboard arranged exactly like the periodic ta-
bles of elements on a wall-chart. As this book is not written for physics experts, however, there is no point in
going into further details of Kapitza's experimental research.

On the more personal side, Kapitza had a comfortable
home, where he lived with his charming wife, Anya, *née*
Krylova. Her father, Alexei Nikolaevich Krylov, the famous Russian mathematician, who before the Russian

Revolution was an admiral of the Imperial Russian Navy, had lived as an émigré in Paris. This unusual combination of activities was due to the fact that as a naval engineer, in order to handle mathematically the vibrations of battleships and their big guns, he had developed the theory of nonlinear differential equations. Later he returned to Russia as a member of the Soviet Academy of Sciences (at that time located in Leningrad), and in 1932 and 1933 I had the honor to serve under him in the academy's Physico-Mathematical Institute, of which he was the director. Being an old sailor, he liked to use harbor slang. I remember numerous occasions when he was presiding at the institute's staff meetings, and had to announce some specially corny request from the academy's dialectical-materialistic cell.

"Marivanovna," he would say to his secretary, the only woman at the meeting, "please stick your thumbs into your ears: I want to express myself." And then he thundered a three-storied docks-and-ports expression.

Being of the old seagoing school, he did not recognize any such innovations as the theory of relativity or the quantum theory. Once he told me that by using the same kind of arguments, he could calculate the distance to the throne of God. In 1905, the year of the Russian-Japanese War, all churches in Mother Russia sent prayers to God to punish the Japanese. But the great Japanese earthquake did not come until 1923, eighteen years later. Assuming that prayers are propagated with the maximum possible velocity, i.e., the velocity of light in a vacuum, and that God's response to just requests would be relayed back to earth at the same speed, one easily finds that the distance to the throne of God is 9 light-years.

But back to his daughter Anya and Peter Kapitza. I sincerely hope that neither of them will scold me for telling this story, because it is too good to be lost to future

generations. Peter met Anya in Paris when he came from
Cambridge to talk to her father. They liked each other,
and he invited her to the opera. During the performance,
he made some jocular remark to her, and she promptly
grabbed his hair and pulled it. Then, to avoid *le scandale,*
they decided to get married, and the next day Kapitza
went to see the Soviet ambassador to arrange matters.

"Sorry, Professor Kapitza," said the ambassador, "you
can marry practically any girl in Paris but not this one;
she has a Nansen passport." [8]

"Very well!" exclaimed Peter, banging his fist on the
table. "I will go back to Cambridge, obtain British citi-
zenship, and marry her anyway!"

"Wait a minute!" begged the scared ambassador. "I will
see what I can do." He grabbed the telephone. "I want to
talk to the ambassador of Iran. . . . Yes, right away! . . .
Your Excellency, this is the ambassador of the Soviet So-
cialist Republics. I would appreciate a favor. I have a girl
here, Mademoiselle Krylova. Nansen passport, you know.
I would appreciate it, if by tomorrow noon she could become a rightful citizen of Iran. . . . Thank you very
much, Your Excellency!"

Well, the next day Kapitza married an Iranian girl who
automatically became a Soviet citizen by marriage!

Now back to nuclear physics. That winter Rutherford
seriously contemplated the possibility of splitting atomic
nuclei, not by bombarding them with alpha particles from
natural radioactive elements but by using ions of various
light elements artificially accelerated in high electric
fields. Indeed this would give a large range of possible
projectiles: in particular, the hydrogen nuclei, protons,

[8] A passport issued by the Nansen International Office for Refugees, created by the League of Nations, and named for Fridtj of Nansen, the Norwegian Arctic explorer and humanitarian.

the lightest of them all. The question was: what energy should be communicated to protons to produce a noticeable yield on the target? Remembering my success in explaining his experiments with alpha bombardment, and being now more disposed toward "these new theories," he asked me if I could make a guess. It was very easy to answer this question. It followed from the theory that the penetrability of the potential barrier surrounding the nucleus was proportional to the atomic number of the bombarded nucleus and to the charge of the projectile, and inversely proportional to its velocity. Thus, since a proton has half of the alpha particle's electric charge, it would produce (in the same bombarded element) about the same effect as an alpha particle traveling at only one-half of the proton's velocity. Since protons are four times less massive than alpha particles, the necessary kinetic energy of a proton to get through the barrier would be $\frac{1}{4} \times (\frac{1}{2})^2 = \frac{1}{16}$ of the alpha particle.

"Is it that simple?" asked Rutherford. "I thought that you would have to cover sheets of paper with your damned formula."

"Not in this case," I said.

Rutherford called in John Cockcroft and Ernest Walton, with whom he had discussed the experimental possibilities beforehand.

"Build me a one-million-electron-volt accelerator; we will crack the lithium nucleus without any trouble," said Rutherford. And so they did. When, later, sitting it out in Leningrad, I was informed of their success, I wired to Cockcroft as follows: "Good stroke, John; good golf-ball protons!"

In the early summer of 1930 there arrived in Cambridge my old friend Dau, and we went for an extensive trip through England and Scotland to see such sights as the old castles and museums. The locomotion was, of

*A difficulty and its resolution: with John Cockcroft (left) at the Cavendish Laboratory.*

course, to be provided by my little BSA, with me at the handlebars and Dau on the back seat.

The academic year at the Cavendish Laboratory had ended, and when I returned from my vacation I was invited by Bohr to spend the winter in Copenhagen. Since my passport was good only for one year it had to be extended for another six months, which was easily arranged at Bohr's request by the Soviet ambassador in Denmark. I do not remember his name, but when I met him later I found that he had started his career as a mathematician and subsequently had joined the diplomatic corps.

During the Christmas holidays Niels Bohr and I went to Norway for a fortnight's skiing trip in the neighborhood of Trondheim. We were to join in Oslo a former student of Bohr, Svin Rosseland, then the director of the university observatory, and the Norwegian atmospheric

*Sports fans in Copenhagen. From left to right: Lev Landau, Aage Bohr, George Gamow, Eric Bohr, and Edward Teller (November 1930).*

physicists big Carl Størmer, *gamle* (old) Bjerknes, and young Solberg, who were studying the aurora borealis.

I was very much amused when our Norwegian friends told me that when I spoke Danish, rudimentary and poor as it was, they could understand me better than they understood Bohr. The real reason was that during a long period (from the late fourteenth century until 1814) when Norway was ruled by the Danes, the population completely lost their original language and began to speak broken Danish. In the process they pronounced Danish words as foreigners would pronounce them—more distinctly and sharply. So did I, as a result of which my Danish sounded more like Norwegian and was easier for the Norwegians to catch than Bohr's guttural speech.

While spoken Danish and Norwegian sound quite different, they are almost identical in written form and, reading a book, one may go through a couple of pages before finding a word the spelling of which permits one to tell whether the book is written in Danish or Norwegian. The only example I remember is the word for girl, which in Danish is spelled *pige* and pronounced as *pee-a*, while the Norwegian spelling is *pikke*, pronounced as *pick-ka*. So much about philology.

Bohr and I arrived in Oslo a couple of days before the planned trip north, and the next morning Rosseland took us, just for practice, to a skiing hill known as Holmenkollen, overlooking the city. We traveled to the top by an electric lift, put on our skis, and came to the starting point. I was used to the *staa paa* ski (in Norway one *stands* on skis, while the skis run) in the Alps, on wide-open snow surfaces above the timberland. But here the situation was quite different: a narrow track with trees on both sides going down and down and down. Bohr went first, Rosseland followed him, and I was the last. I was gliding faster and faster, with tree trunks smashing past

Piz da Daint.
2971 m. ü. M

*Signing a letter to the British scientific journal* Nature, *with Lev Landau at Piz da Daint, Switzerland.*

on both sides of me. In the open snow I would have made a snowplow, but here I did not know what to do. Rosseland told me later that I should have put the sticks between my legs and sat on them. But in the Alps this would certainly not be done, and so it didn't even occur to me. It seemed to me that I was approaching the speed of sound, but before I could say "Mach One" I was down and out. My right knee was badly swollen and aching. The track was deserted and no help was in sight. I sat there remembering the verses written by Zhenya concerning our skiing on the hills (if any) near Leningrad.

> Gee-Gee [9] fell and lost his ski.
> Dimus, Dau, Ksana, Ki! [10]
> Oh, you lazy lads and lasses,
> Find for me in snow my glasses.

I do not know how much time had passed before I saw
Rosseland climbing the hill. The rescue operation was
simple. He carried one of my skis under his right arm,
and I stood on one ski, with my right leg in the air and
my arm around Rosseland's neck. Thus, three-legged, we
skied down. When the doctor came to see my knee in
Rosseland's house, where we were staying, his instructions
were definite: two weeks in the hospital for removing the
fluid, fixing the dislocated kneecap, and healing.

This was when I had my strongest argument with Bohr.
He wanted me to give up the trip to Trondheim, and I
wanted to go along. Finally I won, and the next day we
boarded the train, with me hopping on one foot and
carrying a pair of skis. The first week, of course, I had to
stay in the lodge all day long while the able-legged people
were making various "scenic trips" in the neighborhood.
But this forced confinement was made pleasant by the
presence of the charming daughter of the lodge-owner,
and I had no complaints. For the second week a long
cross-country trip from village to village through comparatively flat country was planned. My knee had healed a little, and I could put weight on my right foot. So I decided
to go along, with an elastic bandage on my knee. I was
helped in this decision by Bjerknes, who told me, "We
two will stick together and take it easy. You are twenty-six
years old and I am sixty-eight; and we both cannot afford

[9] My nickname during that period of life. (The translation of these verses is
my own.)
[10] Oksana Korzukhina and Kira Tunileinen, the two medical coeds in our
skiing and other adventures.

to fall. Let the other people in their forties or fifties go ahead; we will still be back in time for supper."

All that week I was living in a fairyland. Most of each day was dark night, with the sky full of bright stars and a colorful display of polar lights. And, as old Bjerknes promised, each day we reached our destination on time and ready for the tasty *smørrebrød*. We made overnight stops in the houses of peasants who were connected with the research on terrestrial magnetism and were operating various kinds of magnetometers used in these studies.

When I returned to Copenhagen, my knee had im-

*Niels Bohr learning to ride my BSA motorcycle.*

proved quite considerably but, strange as it seems, it both-
ered me more while walking on the city streets than it did
in gliding along the snowy hills. But time did its work,
and although I never again risked standing on skis, I am
glad that I did not go to that hospital in Oslo. In fact, if
during recent years somebody had asked me which knee
was damaged, I probably would not have been able to remember if it was the right or the left one.

But a few days ago I awakened in the morning with a
sharp pain in the right knee. I pulled up my pajama trou-
ser, and there was a bluish-red swelling over the kneecap.
My knee was apparently afraid that I would forget to
mention it in my autobiography (as I probably would
have) and took this measure to remind me about it. When
I telephoned my doctor to make an appointment in his
office to examine my knee, he asked how and when the accident had happened.

"I fell down skiing near Oslo about thirty-eight years
ago," I said.

And when later I came to his office, he was satisfied to
find that my trouble was not psychogenic but really and
truly osteopathic. With a syringe he drew out about 12 cc
of fluid from that swelling, and it now feels much better,
thank you.

# 4

## Last Return to Russia

My return to Russia in the spring of 1931 was a sharp contrast to the bread-and-salt reception [1] that had greeted me on my first trip home, two years earlier. During the previous winter, while in Copenhagen, I had received an invitation from Guglielmo Marconi to attend the first International Congress on the Atomic Nucleus in Rome that fall (*Convegno Nucleare, Roma,* October 1931) and to present a major paper on nuclear structure. Thus I had decided that, instead of returning to Leningrad in the spring, I would spend the summer driving my BSA around Europe, and wind up in Rome by the time of the congress. This would have necessitated, however, another extension of my passport, and I went to the Soviet embassy to arrange it. The ambassador talked to me very nicely and promised to write to Moscow and to arrange matters. A few weeks later I learned that the ambassador wanted to talk to me again. When I came to his office, he said that he had just received an answer from Moscow to his request and that they "quite naturally" wanted to see

[1] It is an old Russian custom to meet an honored guest with a loaf of bread and a cup of salt.

me in Narkompros, after I had been abroad for such a
long period of time, before letting me go again. "I advise
you," said he "to go to the USSR right now, show yourself
in Moscow, spend the summer on the Black Sea or somewhere, and by that time your new passport for the Rome
congress should be ready."

This was rather disappointing, since I had been looking
forward to a nice motorcycle trip through European countries before returning to Leningrad after the congress, via
Istanbul and Odessa, where I could visit my father. But
there was nothing doing, and a few days later I took a direct plane from Copenhagen to Moscow.

Arriving in Moscow, I stayed at the House of Scientists,
a kind of professional club with lodging, cafeteria, library,
and so forth, organized by KSU (the Commission for
Helping Scientists), and shared a room with the children's
verse writer Chukovski, whose work I had always highly
admired.[2] When I went to Narkompros to show Marconi's
invitation and to organize the trip to Italy, I felt right
away that the atmosphere was quite different from what it
had been two years ago. In fact, when I visited friends
from the Moscow University, they looked at me in bewil-
derment, asking why on earth I had come back. "Well,
why not?" was my answer. Then I learned that during the
almost two years of my absence great changes had taken
place in the attitude of the Soviet government toward science and scientists. Whereas earlier in the history of the
post-Revolutionary reconstruction the government was
anxious to re-establish contact with science "beyond the
borders" and was proud of Russian scientists who were invited to scientific gatherings in Western Europe and
America, Russian science now had become one of the
weapons for fighting the capitalistic world. Just as Hitler

[2] As a rule, at least in Russia, really good children's verses and stage plays
leave children cold but appeal to adults.

was dividing science and the arts into Jewish and Aryan camps, Stalin created the notion of capitalistic and proletarian science. It became a crime for Russian scientists to "fraternize" with scientists of the capitalistic countries, and those Russian scientists who were going abroad were supposed to learn the "secrets" of capitalistic science without revealing the "secrets" of proletarian science. Much attention was paid to the maintainance of correct Marxist "ideology" by Russian scientists, as well as by Russian novelists, poets, composers, and artists. Science became subjugated to the official state philosophy of dialectical materialism, used by Marx, Engels, and Lenin in their writings on sociological problems. Any deviation from the correct (by definition) dialectical-materialistic ideology was considered to be a threat to the working class and was severely persecuted.

With very few exceptions, philosophers do not know much science and do not understand it, which is quite natural because science lies beyond the boundaries of typical philosophical subjects such as ethics, aesthetics, and gnosiology. But while in the free countries philosophers are quite harmless, in the dictatorial countries they constitute a great danger for the development of science. In Russia, state philosophers are bred in the Communist Academy in Moscow and are placed in all the educational and research institutions to prevent the professors and researchers from falling into idealistic, capitalistic heresies. The state philosophers are usually somewhat familiar with the subject of the research institution they are going to supervise, being either former schoolteachers or having taken in the academy a one-semester course on the subject in question. But they rank in their power above the scientific directors of the institutions and can veto any research project or publication which deviates from the correct ideology. One notable example of philosophical dictatorship in Russian science was the prohibition of Einstein's theory of relativity on the ground that it denied world ether, "the existence of which follows directly from the philosophy of dialectical materialism." It is interesting to note that the existence of the "world ether" was doubted long before Einstein by Engels, who in one of his letters to friends wrote: ". . . the world ether, if it exists."

Here is a story about the trouble that arose in 1925 when I defended Einstein's point of view, according to which the "world ether" (at least in the sense it was understood in classical physics) does not exist. One day when Dau and I were discussing some problems in the Borgman Library, in came Abatic Bronstein, carrying the newly published volume of the *Encyclopedia Sovietica*. This volume contained the word: *Ether (Light-)*, with a long article written by a certain Gessen. We all knew Comrade Gessen very well; he was the "red director" of the Physics Institute in Moscow University and his job was to see that the "scientific director" (the well-known physicist Professor L. Mandelstamm) and the staff did not deviate into idealistic marshes from the straight path of dialectical materialism. A former schoolteacher, Comrade Gessen knew some physics but was mostly interested in photography and made very good portraits of the pretty coeds. The article began with the introduction in 1690 by Christian Huygens of the notion of light-ether as the carrier of light waves, the difficulties which arose as the result of an unsuccessful attempt in 1887 by A. A. Michelson to detect the motion of the earth through it, and Einstein's rejection of such a universal medium in laying the foundation for his theory of relativity. But, continued Comrade Gessen, Einstein's proposal was unacceptable from the point of view of dialectical materialism. World ether must exist and must possess the properties of all other common material substances. It was the main task of Soviet physicists to

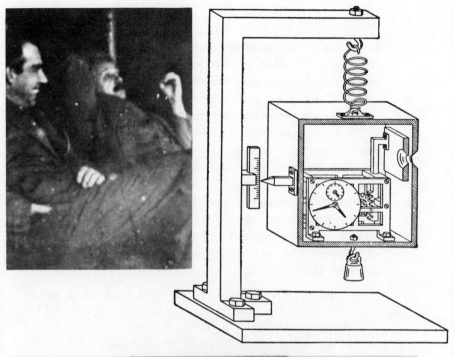

*Bohr and Einstein arguing about the formula $\Delta E \Delta t \geq h$, Einstein's $\Delta E \Delta t$ gadget, and my own, built to help me understand.*

prove the existence of the material light-ether and to find
its true mechanical properties. The idealistic ideas on
which Einstein founded his theory of relativity were con-
trary to the basic principles of Marxism, and therefore
that theory must be rejected. Etc., etc., etc. . . .

We had a good laugh at Gessen's naïve stupidity, and
decided to send him a joking teleletter.[3] I have reproduced it from memory but in good approximation. The
drawing, originally made by Ira (the artist), represented a
tomcat (and Comrade Gessen looked like one) on top of a
trash pile formed by the empty containers of various
"fluids" once introduced and then rejected in the history
of physics. The text, which was, of course, originally in
Russian, read as follows:

> Being inspired by your article on the light-ether, we are
> enthusiastically pushing forward to prove its material ex-
> istence. Old Albert is an idealistic idiot!
> We call for your leadership in the search for caloric,
> flogiston, and electric fluids.
>
> G. Gamow      Z. Genazvali
> L. Landau      S. Grilokishnikov
> A. Bronstein

We expected that Gessen would blow up, but his explosion exceeded by far all our expectations. He took our
teleletter to the Communist Academy in Moscow and accused us of being in open revolt against the principles of
dialectical materialism and the Marxist ideology. As the
result, by orders from Moscow, a "condemnation session"
was organized jointly by Joffe's Roentgen Institute and
the Polytechnic Institute with which it was associated.
We were to be tried as saboteurs of Soviet science. Dau,
Abatic, and the two graduate students who signed the tele-

[3] At that time they had just established between Leningrad and Moscow
a teletype communication system. One could write a letter on a special
blank, and it was transferred by wire in the original handwriting.

*Drawing for the teleletter sent to Comrade Gessen.*

letter had to appear, since they were all doing research at the Roentgen Institute and teaching at the Polytechnic Institute. I did not have to go, since I had a research position with the Physico-Mathematical Institute of the Academy of Sciences and lectured at the university, which had no connection with the Roentgen and Polytechnic Institutes. Apparently it was assumed that I would be "tried" in the Academy of Sciences and the university at a special meeting, which, however, never took place.

After the condemnation meeting, which lasted for
hours, Dau and Abatic came to my apartment and related
what had happened. We were found guilty of anti-Revolu-
tionary activity by a jury of machine-shop workers of the
institute. The two graduate students who signed the tele-
gram lost their stipends and had to leave town. Dau and
Abatic were dismissed from their teaching jobs in the
Polytechnic Institute (to prevent their infecting the minds
of students with poisonous deviationist ideas) but were
retained at their research positions at the Roentgen Institute. Nothing happened to me, since I was not connected
with that outfit. But there were proposals to give us all
"minus five" punishment (a ban on living in the five largest cities of the USSR), which also never materialized.
After the thaw that followed Stalin's death, the Communist Academy issued a proclamation in which it accepted

ACADEMICIAN
ABRAM JOFFE.

THEORETICIAN
JACOB FRENKEL

the validity of Einstein's theory (but, preferably, with the world ether) in recognition of the merits of academician Abram Joffe, Director of the Roentgen Institute, "in the scientifico-technical development of the Soviet Union."

By another decree of the Communist Academy, Heisenberg's matrix mechanics was declared antimaterialistic, and theoretical physicists were ordered to use exclusively Schrödinger's wave mechanics. (A reverse opinion was recently expressed by the famous British physicist P. A. M. Dirac, who thinks that Heisenberg is right and Schrödinger is wrong.) In this connection I had an unpleasant experience when staying in Leningrad from 1931 to 1933. I was asked to deliver in the House of Scientists a popular lecture for a mixed audience on the subject of modern quantum theory. When I started explaining Heisenberg's uncertainty relations, a dialectical materialistic philospher attached to this institution interrupted my lecture and dismissed the audience, and the next week I received strict instructions from my university never to speak again (at least in public) about uncertainty relations. The pressure was temporarily released by an article in *Pravda* written by a high-ranking government official who was apparently more of a practical Communist than a philosophizing dialectical materialist. The article was entitled something like: "Should One Use the Philosophy of Dialectical Materialism in an Instruction Book on How to Catch Crawfish in the Rivers and Lakes of the Soviet Union?"

But while in the physical sciences the interference of the government philosophers was mostly of nuisance value, a real tragedy occurred in the biological sciences, especially in the field of genetics. There appeared a self-proclaimed genius named Comrade Trofim Lysenko, who declared the theory of chromosomal inheritance to be completely wrong and returned to the pre-Mendelian point of view that all changes in living organisms are due to environment, and that all such changes are carried on in the reproductive processes. Lysenko's ideas appealed to the Soviet government of that period, probably mostly because of the denial of any "hereditary treasures" from the pre-Revolutionary years. All human beings are born equal in their abilities, this theory said, provided that they are placed in a suitable environment. "Any charwoman can become the ruler of the state!" was the slogan of the time.

While the existence or nonexistence of the light-carrying ether and the validity or nonvalidity of the quantum-mechanical uncertainty relations had very little influence on the development of the physical sciences and engineering, wrong views concerning the process of heredity are bound to have catastrophic effects on the agrarian development of any country. And that is what happened in Soviet Russia when Lysenko's views were accepted as the basis of the governmental agrarian policies. The "scientific" disagreement turned into a bloody purge, and Russian geneticists were dismissed, jailed, and (probably) executed. The leading Russian geneticist, Nikolai Ivanovich Vavilov, mysteriously disappeared in the summer of 1940, and nobody at that time knew what had happened to him. The development of agriculture and husbandry in the entire country was now based on the wrong "environmental theories" of Lysenko, who became, so to speak, the dictator of the countryside.

It was not until 1955 that the Soviet government first recognized its mistakes, and not until the middle 1960s that Russian genetics came back to life. Here I want to quote from the introduction to *Selected Works of N. I. Vavilov* (2 volumes, 902 pages, published in 1967 by the Science Publishing Agency in Leningrad).

*Drawing of N. I. Vavilov in the two-volume edition of
his selected works, published in Leningrad in 1967, after
his "rehabilitation."*

Beginning in 1932 N. I. Vavilov encountered more and
more difficulties in directing VIR [4] and carrying out his
ideas. After he was dismissed from the position of president [of this institution], all his development plans and
reports sent to the presidium of the VASXNIL [5] were returned with negative answers signed by one of the vice
presidents [Comrade Lysenko?], and the scientific secretary. These answers are preserved in the archives. It was
proposed summarily to N. I. Vavilov that he accept the
new pseudo-scientific theoretical views [in genetics]. Increasing cuts were made in money for his research.

The tragic end of Nikolai Ivanovich was inescapable.
On August 6, 1940, N. I. Vavilov was arrested in Tcherovizi
in the Ukraine [during an agricultural sampling expedi-
tion]. Two and a half years later, on January 26, 1943, he
died [in prison, from hunger]. Only 13 years after that,

[4] All-Union Institute of Horticulture.
[5] Lenin's All-Union Academy of Agricultural Sciences.

in August 1955, Nikolai Ivanovich Vavilov was posthumously restored to favor.

Finally, only in recent years, there has appeared wide scientific and biographical literature about him. A swift, turbulent river of good will, admiration, and worship broke the wall purposely built by irresponsible people of ill will, who were leading their followers in the sinful fanaticism and militant ignorance. As Nikolai Ivanovich often put it: "Of all sicknesses, the most dangerous one is ignorance."

Speaking about Lysenko's theory of environmental changes in the living organism, which is essentially the idea first formulated early in the nineteenth century by the French naturalist Lamarck, I recall my first visit to the University of Colorado, which occurred in about 1951. At that time I was living in Los Alamos, New Mexico, participating in the development of the thermonuclear weapon (hydrogen bomb), and was asked by my old friend Ted Puck, the chairman of the biophysics department in the medical school of the university, to come over and give a talk on what an interested physicist might be thinking about biological problems. I spoke in a large auditorium of the Medical Center in Denver, the place being filled with men and women in white laboratory coats. After discussing Bohr's old and now rejected views, according to which there must exist uncertain relations between detailed knowledge of the internal structure of a cell and of life itself, and Schrödinger's (now flourishing) ideas about the necessity of the intake of "negative entropy" for the continuation of life, I told the audience:

"In conclusion I should like to say a few words about the present conflict in genetics. While Western European countries and the United States continue to hang on to the old Mendelian theory of chromosomal heredity, new revolutionary ideas are generated by the renowned Soviet Russian agriculturalist Comrade Lysenko. According to these new and vigorous ideas, the old theories, insisting that only the changes caused by mutations in chromosomes are carried on by the inheritance process, are completely wrong. Comrade Lysenko insists that all the changes in living organisms are caused by environment and propagate down the generations."

At this point in my speech, I looked at the audience and was terrified. They all looked back at me with disgust (and in some cases pity) in their eyes, and I was afraid that in a few moments I would become the target of flying tomatoes and rotten eggs. Thus I continued:

"It is, of course, true that in many cases a son newly born to Mrs. Doe resembles her husband, John, in accordance with Mendel's ideas. But, on the other hand, it also often happens that the baby looks exactly like Sam Peters, the milkman, where we clearly have the case of Comrade Lysenko's environmental phenomenon."

I actually could not finish the sentence because of the roaring applause on the part of the audience.

Of course, governmental interference in the intellectual life of the country was, and still is, strongly felt in the USSR in literature and other arts. It is enough to mention the case of Pasternak and his novel *Doctor Zhivago*. It is interesting to notice, however, that the "interest" of the ruling class in literature is not characteristic only of the present Communist regime. More than a century ago Alexander Pushkin was exiled by the order of the Czar to the southern Russian provinces for writing a blasphemous poem called "Gavriliade," and such famous writers as Turgenev were prohibited from going abroad, and were confined to their family estates in the country, for their writings.

But I must return to the main topic of these fragments of memory—to the Second Sevastopol Campaign, as I used to call it. After applying for a passport to go to Rome in October, I visited my father in Odessa, spent the rest of the summer on a beach in the Crimea, and returned to Moscow in September to see how things were going. But as I had feared, they were not going well, and I was "fed breakfasts" [6] day after day. Then came the last day on which I should depart in order to arrive in Rome for the first day of meetings, on which my talk was scheduled. Getting another "breakfast," I wired Marconi to shift my talk to the last day of the meeting. But the "breakfasts" continued every morning until it was clear that I could not even make the last day.

"Sorry," said the official in the passport office. "Too bad your passport was delayed."

"But," I said hopefully, "even if I leave tomorrow I will have a chance to talk with my colleagues, since usually everybody stays a few days after the meeting."

"*Nyet*," said the official. "You had better sign this slip, which says that you cancel your application for passport." Thus my paper was read at the meeting by Max Delbrück and published in the proceedings of the congress. I still have a card of condolence sent to me by those who attended, carrying many familiar signatures.

The Roman fiasco had, however, one important consequence in my life. While being "fed breakfasts" in the Moscow passport office, I met a young girl, whom I soon married. She was a physics graduate of Moscow University named Lyubov Vokhminzeva, and was later nicknamed Rho, after the Greek letter. The reason for our marriage was based on the laws of genetics or, one may say, palm-

---

[6] Breakfast, in Russian, is *zavtrak*, which means literally "tomorrow's meal." To be "fed breakfast" is equivalent to being told to inquire again tomorrow.

*The postcard of condolence from the first International Congress on Nuclear Physics (in Rome, October 1931), signed by Marie Curie, Wolfgang Pauli, Samuel Goudsmit, Enrico Fermi, Lise Meitner, F. W. Aston, Robert Millikan, P. M. Blackett, R. H. Fowler, and others.*

*The party in Moscow in the autumn of 1931 at which I
met my first wife, Rho (the girl on whose knees my head
is resting).*

istry. The palms of both my hands show three lines which
have some definite meaning for gypsy fortune-tellers. The
fact is, however, that on both of my hands the two lower
lines never come together, whereas they do so in the great
majority of cases. (Infrequently this happens on only one
hand, but to have it happen on both is really quite rare.)
Well, on both of Rho's palms the lines did not come together either, nor did they, she told me, on her father's
palms. The problem was whether this characteristic is hereditary, and there was only one possible way to find the
answer. And indeed when much later, on the night of
November 4, 1935, I rushed to the maternity ward of the
Women's Hospital in Georgetown, D.C., to see my new-

born son, Rustem Igor, the nurse who brought out the baby was highly surprised when the first thing I did was look at his palms. On both palms the lines *did not* come together.

But the fall of 1931, when I first met Rho, was not the time to carry out genetic studies. It became clear that I, or rather we, were stuck in Russia. Additional proof came soon, when Bohr, worried by my failure to come to Rome, sent me an invitation to visit him in Copenhagen for a few weeks for important discussions on nuclear physics. At that time the Leningrad passport office denied the application on the basis that such a visit would interfere with my lectures at the university.

One of my friends in Moscow who had government connections told me the reason why I had not been permitted to go to Rome. In the year 1931 there was some kind of celebration in the German Academy of Sciences in honor of the philosopher Hegel, who as I have mentioned, was somehow connected with dialectical materialism. Well, the German Academy did not ask the Soviet Academy to send a delegation to this celebration, so, as a retaliation, the Soviet government did not honor my invitation by the Italian Academy. How much truth there is in this version I do not know, but the fact is that an invitation to lecture in the 1932 summer school of the University of Michigan, which did not seem to be connected with any American school of philosophy, did not help me to get the passport either.

# 5

# The Crimean Campaign

Having decided to get out of Russia, Rho and I began to do things quite systematically toward that end, bending over a large map of Soviet Russia with all the border lines clearly shown. Of course, the nearest point to cross the border was Sestroretsk, a bathing beach on the Gulf of Finland less than an hour by train from Leningrad. The Russian-Finnish border lay just north of it, and from the Soviet beach one could observe through binoculars the Finnish bathing beauties in brightly colored bathing suits. (Russian swimming suits at that time were black or a drab brown.) But the narrow strip was thickly populated by guards and dogs and was brightly illuminated at night. On the other hand, the Sino-Russian border in eastern Asia presented fewer manmade obstacles but greater natural ones. In general, the formula, (manmade obstacles) × (natural obstacles) = (a constant), held quite consistently for all the borders.

Then Rho put her finger on the southern tip of the Crimean peninsula and ran it straight south to the bulging shoreline of Turkey. I measured the distance; it was about 170 miles. Not too far at all! Thus started the "Crimean Campaign."

The first idea was to seek the help of smugglers. The Black Sea, called black because it is often very stormy, was always the supply route for the illegal import of foreign goods: French perfume, silk stockings, costume jewelry, and what not. These goods were carried by black-mustachioed Greeks and Turks in small sailboats. I wrote to a friend, an astronomer at Simeis Observatory, which was located not far from Yalta on a high cliff over the blue sea. I said in my letter that I had been recently married and would like to get for my wife some foreign goodies unobtainable in northern Russia, and also a fountain pen for myself if possible.[1] If contact with the smugglers could be established, then next summer we could go for a vacation to the Crimea with enough money to pay for a trip across. The answer was sadly negative. "For several years now," wrote my friend, "we have not been able to get any foreign goods. The Coast Guard has drastically tightened regulations. The fishermen must return to the shore before dark, and, if they have to stay longer, must give in advance detailed information about their expected whereabouts and timing. If a fisherman does not get back on time, his family is severely punished." This was the end of the idea of help from the smugglers.

Since, of course, it was unthinkable to rent any kind of boat, the plan of crossing the Black Sea almost faded out. But then unexpectedly came a new chance. A factory in Moscow began to produce small collapsible boats modeled after the German *Faltboot* used in expeditions for crossing rivers and lakes. We called this boat *baidarka* (see photograph on p. 113). It was made of a rubber hull held in shape by a frame of wooden sticks. When folded,

---

[1] It is interesting to note that in Leningrad's second-hand shops one could buy fountain pens (German-made Montblancs) only during the "season," which was summer. In winter, when foreign visitors wore topcoats, the pens, usually carried in inside pockets of the jacket, could not be so easily snatched in crowded streetcars and buses.

it could be easily transported by two persons, one carrying the packed rubber hull on his back, and the other, the folded stick frame and oars. There was also the "deck sheet" that fitted snugly around the passenger's waist, as in Eskimo kayaks, so that no water could penetrate inside the boat if the waves rolled over it. We found this feature very useful in practice, when a storm started on the second day of our trip and big waves were smashing against our tiny abode. The whole contraption was very light, and Rho and the boat together weighed less than I.

But it was not at all easy to get such a boat to take with us to the Crimea. I managed to get one somehow through the sportsmen's group of the House of Scientists; they arranged for me a factory order for the purpose of "trying the boat out under open-sea conditions."

This standard equipment was supplemented by several additional safety items. Two inflated football bladders were attached inside the boat at the bow and at the stern to make it float even if it were to turn over. Each of us had a rubber cushion attached by shoulder straps. This served as a soft pad against the hard wooden backrest of the boat, and could also serve as a lifebelt. We also carried a handpump to get out any water that might penetrate the inside of the boat in spite of its "hermetic" cover.

An important item was the food supply for the trip, which, we figured, would last five or six days. With the food shortage in Leningrad, we could not, of course, get any special compact high-calorie food. Since there were still a few months before we could go to the Crimea, we started hoarding eggs which sometimes appeared at the market with the stamp "Export." These were eggs earmarked for sale abroad but not accepted there. We hardboiled them and saved them for the trip. We also managed to get several "bricks" of hard "cooking" chocolate, and two bottles of brandy, which turned out to be very handy when we were wet and cold at sea.

The problem of navigation was solved very simply. We had to move straight south. I carried a pocket compass and at night would keep the polar star right over the stern of the boat. I also calculated that when we were halfway to the Turkish shore, Ai Petri, the highest mountain on the Crimean shore, about 5000 feet high, should just disappear below the northern horizon, and soon thereafter the mountains of Asia Minor should appear in the south.

I had a minor argument with Rho, who insisted that we carry tooth powder and two toothbrushes, and I do not remember whether we had them with us or not.

All this sounds very childish, and in fact we behaved very irresponsibly throughout the whole affair. But the fact is that, had the storm not come on the second day of our journey across the Black Sea, we would probably have made the Turkish shore and, incidentally, a world record.

Yes, and one word about documents. All I carried along was my old (and long expired) Danish motorcycle driving license. The plan was that when we reached the Turkish shore I would attempt to explain that we were Danes and ask to be delivered to the Danish Embassy in Istanbul. From there I would telephone to Niels Bohr in Copenhagen, and he would arrange matters.

Now came the problem of the jumping-off point in the Crimea, and here again the House of Scientists turned out to be of great help. In Russia at that time, and probably also now, one could not go to a bathing or other resort and rent a room in a hotel or a motel. There weren't any, except for foreigners. But the KSU maintained a number of vacation bases at the seashores, in the mountains, and elsewhere. The KSU had, among other places, a beautiful Crimean "base" not far from Yalta; it used to be the man-

sion of some rich man of pre-Revolutionary times. It was
located on a beach, had dormitories for men, dormitories
for women, a large dining room, and tennis courts. Scientific workers could obtain, with luck, a *putiovka* (a pass)
for a thirty-day vacation in one of these places, including
transportation, lodging, and food.

Since husbands and wives usually worked in different
scientific establishments, they often spent their vacations
in different places at different times, but this was considered to contribute to the completeness of the vacation.
Although when I married Rho she was working as an optical engineer in a large Moscow factory,[2] she was unem-
ployed when we were planning our trip to the Crimea.
Thus I could not get a bed for her in the women's dormi-
tory of KSU's base and she had to rent a room in a *saklia*
(peasant's house) in the nearby village. The original native population of the Crimea were Tartars, people of the
Moslem faith, and the native villages are very picturesque,
with old mosques and *dukhans* (eating places) which serve
shashlik, baklava, and excellent local wines. But my wife
had permission to use all the other facilities of the KSU
base, and in particular to take all her meals with me.

Arriving in the Crimea in the early summer of 1932, we
stored the boat with a fisherman on a beach so that we
could use it whenever we wanted to. And we used it quite
a bit for going along the shoreline, "trying it out under
open-sea conditions." One thing we found out was that it
was more rational to take turns in paddling, rather than
paddling together, since in the latter case the speed of the
boat did not increase by a factor of two. Thus it was finally settled that on the long-range trip across the Black

[2] By the way, in order to get a release from that job and to move to Leningrad she had to present to her factory officials documents proving that
my salary in Leningrad was higher than hers in Moscow. Otherwise, I
would have had to ask for my transfer to Moscow to live with her.

Sea each of us would paddle half an hour while the other was resting.

The problem now was when to start. There was a full moon, and it seemed irrational to wait two weeks for dark nights. The weather was excellent and the sea as smooth as a mirror. We had no way to get any weather forecasts; such things were secret, and any inquiries could arouse suspicion. Thus one evening we brought down our food supply and loaded it into the boat, and the next morning after breakfast we pulled the boat into the water and were off. We told everyone at the base, as well as the early birds on the beach who waved us off, that we were going to the Simeis Observatory and would stay there overnight, so

*Rho and I in our boat on the Black Sea in the Crimea.*

that there would be no alarm when we did not show up
for the evening meal. First we followed the shoreline toward Simeis but, as soon as we got out of sight of the
base's beach, we turned the boat straight south.

The first day was a complete success, and the boat slid
fast and gracefully over the smooth waters. In the late afternoon, when the coast range was still clearly showing on
the horizon, a gentle breeze began to blow from the east,
and the water's surface became slightly wavy. But what
was bothering us was not the waves but a school of por-
poises swimming joyfully around our boat, probably taking it for another porpoise of a somewhat different breed.
I will never forget the sight of a porpoise seen through a
wave illuminated by the sun sinking below the horizon. I
photographed it, but the picture was never developed because later the camera and the film were completely
soaked in the water accumulated in the boat.

As soon as the sun sank below the horizon, the full
moon came up in the opposite direction, and soon the
stars appeared in the darkening sky. When the night fell
we felt quite cheerful but rather tired, and here we com-
mitted the first deviation from the original plan; this did
not matter anyway, considering what followed. We had
planned to move continuously throughout the night, one
of us paddling while the other dozed. But we both were
tired, the boat resembled a cradle on the rolling waves,
and, after finishing a bag of fresh strawberries which we
had taken with us, we both fell asleep, leaning back in our
seats.

We woke up before sunrise, only to find that the wind
was stronger and the waves were less gentle. The moon
sank under the horizon and the red sun came up. The
waves were coming from the east and since we were going
south we had to take them on the port side. But there was
a simple way to keep the boat from turning over: all one

had to do was to make a stronger stroke with the paddle
on the off-wind side of the boat when the next wave was
coming. Thus we were still proceeding south, even
though perhaps at a slower speed.

However, toward the evening of that day the situation
became considerably worse. The wind was stronger and
blew the foam from the crests of the incoming waves, forc-
ing us to turn the boat eastward to face the waves. From
that time on I had to take complete responsibility, since
Rho was not strong enough to handle the paddle. The
bow of the boat rose on each wave and then flapped back
into the trough when the crest passed. When I was not
careful enough to keep the boat straight, the wave and
foam rolled over the "deck," slashing into my face (I had
to use the front seat, since there was more space for my
long legs). But Rho was also very busy pumping out the
water that penetrated inside the boat each time a wave
rolled over. The rowing served only to keep the boat in
the correct position with respect to the waves, but not at
all for propelling it. In fact, I was surprised to see a piece
of rope tied to the bow pointing forward as if it were a
bowsprit. The force of the wind pressing against my chest
was moving the boat backward, stern first. As I figured
out later, the wind was blowing us northwestward and toward the shore.

Sometime during the night the wind suddenly stopped,
the white crests disappeared, and the sea's surface again assumed a pattern of long rolling waves. The light of the
full moon reflected from the water made the surface look
like the floor of a large cathedral made of black and white
marble stone in a chessboard pattern. Being tired of sitting, I almost thought of getting out of the boat and walking on that smooth marble floor. Fortunately I did not try
it. In another hallucination, we both saw long wooden
sticks rising out of the water, and even discussed whether

we should hold on to one if we came to it. Rho was talking irrationally about some skipper of a schooner who suggested taking us aboard.

Anyway, I was able again to control the motion of the
boat, rowing this time straight toward the polar star. It
was still dark when we saw the shoreline, a high rocky
cliff coming vertically down into the water. There was no
possibility of landing there, but we thought there might
be a beach to the right or to the left. I turned right, and
that was a lucky choice because, as I learned later, the cliff
continued for miles in the westerly direction. And then
we saw a tiny sandy beach. There appeared to us to be
two wooden sticks some fifty feet apart rising from the
water between us and the shore, but we decided that this
was just another hallucination. I headed right between
them and got into a fisherman's net supported by these
sticks, pulled back, and finally the bow of the boat
touched the sand. We scrambled out, pulled the boat out
of the water, drank some of the brandy, and collapsed into
sleep on the sand.

When we woke up, the sun was high above the horizon
and I saw several Tartar fishermen standing in bewilder-
ment looking at us. I tried to get on my feet, but fell back
on the sand. I just could not keep my equilibrium. We
explained to the fisherman that we had been blown offshore by the night breeze, and they took us first to their
village and then to a hospital in the nearby city, Bala-
klava, some seventy miles west of Alupka, from which we
had sailed for Turkey. After recuperating in the hospital
for a couple of days, we were driven back to the KSU
base. Our boat came with us, with all its contents except
the bottles of brandy, which the fishermen held for their
services. We did not use the boat again on the Black Sea,
but when we brought it back to Leningrad, we tried it
out again on the Neva River. But it was a windy day, and

we headed in a hurry to the nearest landing point to get out of it. I later returned it to the sports club of the House of Scientists, with the report that it was excellent under open-sea conditions except in a rough sea. But the sea had been really rough during our trip, and in fact I found after returning to the KSU base that a small steamboat which served a chain of resorts along the south shore of the Crimea was not operating on that day because of the difficulties of coming to the landing stockades.

When we were brought to the KSU base from the hospital, we told the story of being blown offshore by the night breeze, and it was accepted as an official version. I do not know how many people really believed it, but on the other hand, I truly cannot see how people could think that we were actually heading for Turkey. But I still believe that we could have made it if the weather had been nice.

# 6

## The Solvay Congress

In the beginning of the twentieth century a group of Russian biologists organized a marine-life observation station at the entrance to a fiord of the Arctic Ocean, deep in which is located the ice-free port Murmansk. As the years went by, this little spot, named Polar Village, developed into an important scientific center similar to the Marine Biological Laboratory at Woods Hole in Massachusetts, even though not as popular because of a considerably less pleasant climate.

Polar Village attracted our attention because of its location close to the Norwegian border. Indeed, if one borrowed (or stole) one of the motorboats used for the collection of biological samples, one could "easily" make a run to the Norwegian side of the border.

The vicinity of Murmansk was familiar to us from previous experience. During the Christmas vacation of 1932 we spent a couple of weeks at the KSU base in Khibini, a little Karelian village on the railroad from Leningrad to Murmansk. This was, of course, in the midst of the long polar night with a beautiful display of aurora borealis. We had our skis with us, and had planned to cross the

Finnish border on skis or, still better, to hire an Eskimo with a sleigh and reindeer who would drive us, in Santa Claus fashion, across the forbidden line. Nothing came of that plan. The ski trip would have been almost beyond human endurance, and we also found upon arrival that all the natives approached by prospective trans-border travelers were permitted to keep all the money paid to them for the "transportation," plus an additional amount to be paid them by the border officials into whose hands the tourists were to be delivered. Thus the winter trip became nothing but a rather fancy Christmas vacation.

The motorboat plan seemed to be more promising, and so I wrote to one of the biologists whom I knew in Polar Village, saying that we would like to visit it sometime in July. But before going to that destination we decided to stay for a week or so at the KSU base in Khibini to see how it looked in the daytime. Dau decided to go with us, even though he was not interested in border-crossing. He was always an ardent Marxist, but along Trotskyite lines. When he was visiting Copenhagen or Cambridge while I was there, he always wore a red blazer as the symbol of his Marxist views, which made him look respectively like a Danish mailman or an English postbox. He used to say that, bad as it might be temporarily in Soviet Russia, it was certainly worse in the capitalist countries and that it made him sick to look at the "bulging muscles" of a German Schutzmann or a British bobby. But he went along with us to Khibini just for the trip. The eternal day gave us more freedom to study the landscape and do some hiking; on one occasion we were almost lost on a trip up the Small White River which took us almost three days (seventy-two hours by wrist-watch).

When Dau left us to go back to Leningrad, we took the train to Murmansk, and then a motorboat from the Marine Station brought us to our final destination. The place was very interesting and the people were very nice, but we came at exactly the wrong time. The Soviet Navy was establishing submarine bases at the entrance of the fiord, and it certainly did not want any biologists hanging around. While I was delivering to the staff of the station my first lecture on the theory of polar lights, I think it was two security officers who walked into the meeting hall and arrested the director (and founder) of the station, who was accused of subversive activities. I do not remember his name, but I do remember his long white beard and the sad look in his eyes when he was led out of the lecture room. The station was to be closed, and so, again defeated, we decided to go back to Leningrad.

A few days after arriving home, I received a letter from Narkompros informing me that I had been delegated by the Soviet government to attend the international Solvay Congress on Nuclear Physics which was to take place in Brussels in October of that year (1933). I could not believe my eyes, but there was an official letter in my hands saying that I must come to Moscow and collect my passport, the necessary visas, and the railroad ticket, a few days prior to my departure.

This brought about a very difficult psychological situation. I had always felt that I did not want to desert my native country, and that as long as I was permitted to travel beyond the Soviet borders and keep in contact with world science, I would always come back home. I could not possibly accept the theory of the alleged hostility between "proletarian" and "capitalist" science; it just did not make any sense to me. Also, the increasing pressure of the dialectical-materialist philosophy was too strong, and I did not want to be sent to a concentration camp in Siberia because of my views about the world ether, the quantum-mechanical uncertainty principle, or chromosomic heredity —which could have happened in due course.

To go to Brussels meant staying abroad, and I was not willing to do so unless Rho was with me. Thus the problem was to get a second passport, or to disobey the government's orders and not attend the Solvay Congress.

The only high-standing government official who could help me with my problem was Nikolai Bukharin, an old revolutionary and a close friend of the late Lenin, as well as the only leading Communist (except, of course, Lenin himself) who came from an old Russian family. I met him when he was on his way down, holding a comparatively minor position as president of a committee supervising the development of Soviet science and engineering, which, of course, had no political importance.[1] Once, he attended my lecture at the Academy of Sciences (at that time still in Leningrad) on thermonuclear reactions and their role in the energy production in the sun and other stars. After this talk he suggested that I head a project for the development of controlled thermonuclear reactions (and that in 1932!). I would have at my disposal for a few minutes one night a week the entire electric power of the Moscow industrial district to send it through a very thick copper wire impregnated with small "bubbles" of lithium-hydrogen mixture. I decided to decline that proposal, and I am glad I did because it certainly would not have worked.

Well, I went to Moscow to see him, and he told me that all he could do for me was to arrange an interview with Vyacheslav Molotov, who was at that time the President of the USSR. I stayed in Moscow with Rho's parents and within a few days was informed that I should appear at a certain hour in the morning at the main gates of the Kremlin. So I did, and was duly escorted to Molotov's office; he was sitting behind the same desk at which Lenin used to sit. There was a short conversation concerning

[1] Bukharin fell a victim of Stalin's purges and was executed five years after I left Russia.

what I was going to talk about at Brussels, and then Molotov asked me why I had come to see him (although, of
course, he knew this very well). I told him that I wanted
to take my wife with me to the Solvay Congress. "But," he
said, "you are going just for two weeks. Can't you be separated from her for that short a time?"

Here I told him the truth, nothing but the truth, but
not the whole truth. "You see," I said, "to make my request persuasive I should tell you that my wife, being a
physicist, acts as my scientific secretary, taking care of papers, notes, and so on. So I cannot attend a large congress
like that without her help. But this is not true. The point
is that she has never been abroad, and after Brussels I
want to take her to Paris to see the Louvre, the *Folies
Bergère,* and so forth, and to do some shopping."

He smiled, made a note on his pad, and told me to
come back a week or so before I would have to leave, adding, "I don't think this will be difficult to arrange."

I walked out of the Kremlin dancing and, childish as it
was, stopped in a picture store and bought a framed por-
trait of Molotov to hang over my desk.

But when I came back to Moscow in October I was
met by an official from the Secretariat who told me that
my case had been considered and that it had been decided
that I had better go alone.

"But Comrade Molotov told me that this could easily
be arranged," I protested. "Why the change?"

"You see," he explained, "if we let your wife go with
you to the congress it will establish a precedent, and wives
of all the other scientists would want to go along too. And
this would make things very complicated."

"But Comrade Molotov . . ." I began again. "Well,
may I talk to him?"

"No, he is on vacation in Southeast Asia, hunting tigers.

You had better go to the passport office and get all the necessary documents."

"No," I said, "I will not. I am not going to Brussels."

"But you *have* to go, you are the representative of the Soviet Union."

Well, I was of course acting insanely; one does not talk like that to Soviet officials.

"You can send me as far as the Soviet border under guard," I said, "but the guards will not be permitted to escort me to Brussels and force me to take my seat in the congress hall."

I turned on my heels and went out. I stayed a few more days in Moscow, awaiting arrest. The very next day the telephone rang. It was somebody from the passport office informing me that I should come to pick up my passport.

"Is the second passport ready too?" I asked.

"No, only one."

"Then please telephone me when both passports are ready. Why should I walk to your office twice?"

The next day and the day after, the same telephone conversation took place. Then on the fourth day the voice on the telephone informed me that both passports were ready. And indeed they were! I took the overnight train to Leningrad and the next morning visited the Finnish and Danish consulates to obtain transit visas, and, after attending the afternoon performance of the ballet *Koniok Gorbunok* (Little Hunchback Horse), Rho and I boarded the train for Helsingfors on the way to Copenhagen and Brussels!

Thinking back now, I still cannot figure out how it happened that I got the second passport. It seems most likely to me that the wires had crossed somewhere. It is possible that my rather "unconventional" behavior in the Kremlin office, caused by the strain of the moment, had much to do with it. I had to go to Brussels, to maintain friendly scientific relations between the USSR and France, and here I refused to go . . .Well, I do not know.

The meeting of the XIIIth Solvay Congress passed more or less uneventfully, except for an open revolt in the beginning of my presentation when both French and non-French physicists demanded that I change from speaking French to English. I had a minor disappointment in not being able to attend a dinner given by King Albert for the participants in the congress. The invitation called for "white tie," and I did not possess even a "black tie," nor yet even a decent black suit. I inquired in all places where dress clothes could be rented, but could not find my size; everything available was too small. Thus, regretfully, I had to decline King Albert's hospitality and have dinner elsewhere.

The next time I was invited to the Solvay Congress was for a meeting scheduled for October 1939. I planned well ahead and had nice evening attire specially made for me in Washington. But I also missed this dinner, in this case with King Leopold, because the Germans attacked Poland, and not only was the congress canceled but so were all sailings to Europe.

My chance came again in the fall of 1958. The congress in June of that year was dedicated to the "Structure and Evolution of the Universe." I received a letter from Pauli, who was on the organization committee, asking me whether I would like to be invited. I answered with an enthusiastic yes, adding that by a lucky coincidence I would be in Europe anyway that summer, arriving by the *Ile de France* just in time to go to Brussels and have dinner with King Baudouin. Some time later I received another letter from Pauli saying rather sheepishly that he had written to Sir William Bragg, chairman of the congress, proposing that he send me an invitation, but that

Schrödinger  Onnes/Langevin  A. Piccard  P. Debye  Niels Bohr  Wrzymkowsky  Pauli  E. Bauer  P. Ehrenfest  I. Langmuir  Heisenberg  Dirac  Chadwick  Meitner  Kramers  Rutherford  D. Joffé  E. Herzen  T. de Donder  de Broglie  E. Schrödinger  Maurin

*Niels Bohr and Ernest Rutherford at the 1933 Solvay Congress. (Rutherford's face is blurred by smoke from his pipe.)*

Bragg had written back that he would not do so because there were no more vacancies for that meeting. I was not surprised (though somewhat disappointed) about the outcome, since I was an opponent of the steady-state theory. Thus I missed dinner with a third Belgian king.

According to Edward Teller, it is not surprising that the steady-state theory is so popular in England, not only because it was proposed by its three (native-born and imported) sons H. Bondi, T. Gold, and F. Hoyle, but also because it has ever been the policy of Great Britain to

## NEW GENESIS

In the beginning God created radiation and ylem. And ylem was without shape or number, and the nucleons were rushing madly over the face of the deep.

And God said: "Let there be mass two." And there was mass two. And God saw deuterium, and it was good.

And God said: "Let there be mass three." And there was mass three. And God saw tritium and tralphium, and they were good. And God continued to call number after number until He came to transuranium elements. But when He looked back on his work He found that it was not good. In the excitement of counting, He missed calling for mass five and so, naturally, no heavier elements could have been formed.

God was very much disappointed, and wanted first to contract the Universe again, and to start all over from the beginning. But it would be much too simple. Thus, being almighty, God decided to correct His mistake in a most impossible way.

And God said: "Let there be Hoyle." And there was Hoyle. And God looked at Hoyle . . . and told him to make heavy elements in any way he pleased.

And Hoyle decided to make heavy elements in stars, and to spread them around by supernovae explosions. But in doing so he had to obtain the same abundance curve which would have resulted from nucleosynthesis in ylem, if God would not have forgotten to call for mass five.

And so, with the help of God, Hoyle made heavy elements in this way, but it was so complicated that nowadays neither Hoyle, nor God, nor anybody else can figure out exactly how it was done.

Amen.

*My attitude toward the steady-state theory, expressed in this piece, may account for my not receiving an invitation to the 1958 Solvay Congress on cosmology.*

maintain the *status quo* in Europe. Now that the steady-state theory seems to be out of date, I might have a chance to be invited, but there are no Solvay Congresses on cosmology planned. This puts me in the position of a man who dreamed that he was served the famous and delicious dish of *kissel s molokom* (in Russian), or *rød grøde med fløde* (in Danish), which can be described only vaguely in English as something like cranberry sauce with cream. In his dream the man could not eat the *kissel* because he had no spoon. And so the following night he put a large spoon under his pillow, but the dream never returned.

After the XIIIth Solvay Congress I wrote a letter from Brussels to the University of Michigan at Ann Arbor, asking whether my invitation for the summer school, which I could not accept in 1932, could be renewed for the summer of 1934, and when the congress was over and most of the delegates moved to Paris "to have some rest," I got an affirmative answer.

Then came the problem of how to live through the winter, and I talked to Bohr about it. "But Gamow," he said, "you cannot do this. You have to go back to Russia." And then I learned how my "miraculous" exit from the USSR had been organized. Bohr, being worried about my detention in Russia, and being sure that a mere invitation to attend the congress would not help me to get a passport, turned for help to Langevin. Professor Paul Langevin, a famous French physicist and, I suppose, a member of the French Communist Party, was serving as the chairman on the French side, of the Franco-Russian Scientific Cooperation Committee. At the same time he was a permanent member of the committee that organized the Solvay Congresses. Instead of sending the invitation to me, as he normally would have done, he wrote directly to Moscow, asking the government to appoint me as a dele-

gate to the XIIIth Solvay Congress, which started the series of events I have already described

"You have to go home, Gamow," argued Bohr, "because
Langevin did all this at my request and on my responsibility." I felt terrible. Of course there is a good French expression, *noblesse oblige,* but on the other hand, I had arranged for my wife's passport all by myself!

It happened that on this particular day we had been invited for dinner at the home of Madame Marie Curie,
and, sitting next to her at the table, I told her my trou-
bles.

"*Bien,*" she said. "I will talk to Langevin tomorrow."

Before this dinner ended I learned one more thing
about the French language, which I speak "fluently" with
very good pronunciation and very bad grammar. When
the coffee was served I was telling the people at the table,
among them Irène and Fred Joliot-Curie, François Perrin,
and a few other French physicists, about the customs of
German student corporations (fraternities) that I had
learned about from spending the summer in Göttingen.
In order to enter the corporation, the candidate had to do
some public stunt, and the favorite task was to kiss a
bronze statue of a peasant maiden in the fountain at the
city's marketplace. There was always a *Schutzmann* on
duty there, and to distract his attention from the fountain
while the stunt was performed, a pair of helpers used to
stage a fist fight at the far corner of the square. Since the
bronze peasant maiden held a big jug under one arm and
a goose under the other, and since water flowed freely
from both, the student who passed the test used to come
out wet even if he managed to escape arrest.

I was telling this story in French, a language full of hidden pitfalls. When I wanted to say that the boy had *to kiss*
the bronze maiden, I naturally assumed that this verb is

derived from the noun *a kiss*. Since I knew that French
for *a kiss* is *un baiser*, I thought that the verb would be
*baiser*. Little did I know that in the long history of the
French language the verb *baiser* used in this way had become a description of a far more intimate relationship between a man and a woman. In modern French, in speaking
about kissing, one must use the verb *embrasser*, and I am
not sure what one uses for simple embracing.

When I said that *le garçon doit baiser la jeune fille*, si-
lence fell over the dining table. Then Fred Joliot-Curie remarked, *"Ah! Ça serait très difficile!"* and everybody broke
into roars of laughter. But my heart was heavy, and all I
could think about was the conversation between Madame
Curie and Paul Langevin, due to take place the following
morning.

The next day I was sitting in the library of the Sor-
bonne's Pierre Curie Institute, of which Madame Curie
was a director, trying to read some current magazines
which did not seem to make any sense to me. Hours
passed, and finally Madame Curie came in.

"Gamow," she said, putting her hand on my shoulder,
"I have talked to Langevin. You can stay here."

This was my release from *noblesse oblige,* and everything was all right now.


There was a rumor at that time that my decision not to
return home resulted in the detention in Russia of Peter
Kapitza, who was there that summer. This is definitely
not true.

The roots for the detention of Kapitza during his visit
to Russia in 1934 go much farther back in time. Ever
since Kapitza, who originally left Russia as an inconspic-
uous young physicist, had become noted for his work in
Cambridge, the Soviet government had wanted him back.
When, after a long stay in England, he first went back to

Russia by invitation of the Soviet government, Rutherford wrote as a precautionary measure to the Soviet ambassador at the Court of St. James's, asking for assurance
that Kapitza would be back in Cambridge "by September
of this year." The assurance was given, and Kapitza came
back to Cambridge on the dot. The same procedure was
followed for all his subsequent visits except the last one.
In this case Kapitza told Rutherford that such a "letter of
guarantee" was not needed, since he was quite sure that
he would not be detained. He added that one of the high
Soviet officials had told him something like this: "Look
here. You must see by now that nobody wants to hold you
here by force. And it is somewhat beneath our dignity to
give such assurances to the stuffy British lord, who does
not understand these matters."

Thus Kapitza went to Russia, this time with his wife,
his car, and great vacation plans, but without the "guarantee."

When Kapitza was denied permission to return to Cambridge in October 1934, the University of Michigan summer session had ended and I had just arrived in Washington, D.C., as a visiting professor at George Washington
University. I registered as a Soviet citizen in the consulate
service of the Soviet embassy and applied for the continuation of my passport until the following summer. In fact,
during that winter Rho and I kept up contact with the
consulate, and even went to movies with some of its members, criticizing the Hollywood productions. The case of
Kapitza only strengthened my decision not to return to
Leningrad.

But before leaving Europe for the summer session at
Ann Arbor, I had the problem of how to live through the
winter, which was easily solved. My time was divided into
three periods: a two-month fellowship at the Pierre Curie
Institute, two months in the Cavendish Laboratory, and

two months with Bohr in Copenhagen. In the early summer we sailed for New York on the tiny Danish ship
called the *United States* (not to be confused with the present ocean liner of that name).

While in Ann Arbor I received an offer of a professorship at George Washington University. An amusing detail
is that when in Cambridge I did not have enough money
to make the deposit for the transatlantic tickets and had
to borrow some money from Rutherford. Later, in Copenhagen, I again had to borrow money, this time from Bohr,
in order to pay the balance. After I had received several
monthly paychecks from George Washington University,
I saved enough to pay my debts and went to a post office

*A meeting in Copenhagen in the spring of 1934.*

to get two foreign money orders. But the postal clerk, who was evidently not a physicist, was not impressed by either of the names. I am still sorry that I did not save the slips, which were certainly "suitable for framing."

And so, in this impecunious fashion, I began my life in the United States.

# Afterword:

# Notes on My Life in

# the United States[1]

It seems reasonable to divide my activities during the thirty-five years which I have spent in the United States into three separate packages: 1) scientific research; 2) military consultation; and 3) popular book-writing.

## SCIENTIFIC RESEARCH

One of the arrangements I made with Dr. Floyd Heck Marvin, the president of George Washington University, when accepting the professorship, was that another theoretical physicist of my choice would also be invited, so that I would have a chance to discuss problems with someone. This man was, of course, Edward Teller, a Hungarian-born physicist who at that time held a temporary position in England. A number of years ago an article in a national magazine described my contribution to the development of the hydrogen bomb as that of bringing Edward Teller to this country; there is, of course, a shaker of salt

[1] EDITOR'S NOTE: This section, written shortly before Dr. Gamow's death, is essentially only a sketch of what he would have written, had he lived to complete it.

in that statement. But during the prewar years Edward and I were occupied with the more peaceful activities of studying "nonfissionable" nuclei.

Probably our most important contribution to nuclear physics at that period was the formulation of what is now known as the Gamow-Teller selection rule for beta decay, which is a little too abstract to explain in simple words. It boils down essentially to the question as to how an electron leaves the nucleus in the process of beta transformation—whether it goes straight out along the radius vector or follows a hyperbolic trajectory. Enrico Fermi, who originated the theory of beta transformations, accepted the first possibility, but Teller and I found that Fermi's assumption was wrong. It turned out, in fact, that in many cases the beta particle can just as easily escape the nucleus moving along the hyperbolic trajectory. But to do so the electron must "flip over its spin," a fact which gave some important hints concerning the magnetic interaction between the electron and the nucleus.

The work on the Gamow-Teller selection rule was my last major contribution to the field of "pure" nuclear physics, since I was getting more and more interested in the application of nuclear physics to astrophysical phenomena. During these years the experimental knowledge concerning artificial nuclear transformations caused by a proton impact was accumulating at a high rate, and I felt that it was time to revise the early attempts of Houtermans and Atkinson to explain the energy production in the sun and other stars by thermonuclear reactions caused by very high temperatures. Thus, Teller and I decided that in the spring of 1938 the conference on theoretical physics organized annually by George Washington University and the Carnegie Institution of Washington would be devoted to the problems of thermonuclear sources in stars. Among the invited theoretical physicists and astro-

physicists was Hans Bethe, who on his arrival knew
nothing about the interior of stars but everything about the
interior of the nucleus. The conference was very interesting and exciting, and toward the end of it Bethe came out
with a possible scheme of nuclear reactions involving hydrogen and carbon which could produce just enough energy to explain the observed radiation of the sun. Upon
his return to Cornell University, he brushed up the details of that process, and it became what is now known as
the famous carbon cycle.

Shortly before that conference, my former graduate student Charles Critchfield proposed another energy-producing process called the proton-proton reaction (H-H),
which begins with a collision between two protons which
then form a deuteron (a nucleus of heavy hydrogen) by
emitting a positive electron and a neutrino. In calculating
the rate of this process, Charles ran into a mathematical
difficulty and could not get the final result. When he told
this to Hans Bethe, the latter straightened out the difficulty, and the H-H reaction became competitive to the
carbon cycle. In fact, we now know that, in the case of the
sun, the H-H reaction and not the carbon cycle plays the
dominant role. The same is true for all stars fainter than
the sun, whereas for brighter stars, such as Sirius, the carbon cycle is dominant.

The summer of 1939 I spent with my family vacationing on the Copacabana beach in Rio de Janeiro. One evening, visiting the famous Casino da Urca to watch the
gamblers, I was introduced to a young theoretical physicist born on an Amazon River plantation, named Mario
Schoenberg. We became friends, and I arranged for him a
Guggenheim fellowship to spend a year in Washington to
work with me in nuclear astrophysics. His visit was very
successful, and we hit upon a process which could be responsible for the vast stellar explosions known as super-

novae. The trick is done by alternative absorption and re-emission of one of the thermal electrons in the very hot (billions of degrees!) stellar interior by various atomic nuclei. Both processes are accompanied by the emission of neutrinos and antineutrinos which, possessing tremendous penetrating power, pass through the body of the star like a swarm of mosquitoes through chicken wire and carry with them large amounts of energy. Thus the stellar interior cools rapidly, the pressure drops, and the stellar body collapses with a great explosion of light and heat.

All this is too complicated to explain in nontechnical words, and I am mentioning it only as background for how we came to give that process its name. We called it the Urca Process, partially to commemorate the casino in which we first met, and partially because the Urca Process results in a rapid disappearance of thermal energy from the interior of a star, similar to the rapid disappearance of money from the pockets of the gamblers on the Casino da Urca. Sending our article on the Urca Process for publication in *The Physical Review*, I was worried that the editors would ask why we called the process "Urca." After much thought I decided to say that this is short for "unrecordable cooling agent," but they never asked. Today there are other known cooling processes involving neutrinos which work even faster than the Urca Process. For example, a neutrino pair can be formed instead of two gamma quanta in the annihilation of a positive and a negative electron.

The next adventure in astronomy was related to the so-called *white dwarf stars,* highly collapsed stellar bodies the density of which is about a million times greater than the density of water. These white dwarfs represent the end of a star's evolution, when it is completely deprived of internal energy sources that keep the normal stars, like our sun, blown up and shining. They are actually stellar cadavers and are still warm only because they have not had enough time to cool. Given enough time they will lose all their heat and turn into "black dwarfs," the dark, massive bodies traveling aimlessly through the space of the universe. The first discovered white dwarf was the companion of Sirius, also known as Sirius B. While the main star (Sirius A) is 3.5 times more massive and 26 times brighter than the sun, Sirius B has almost the same mass as the sun but is 300 times fainter. The main point, however, is that, although as massive as the sun, Sirius B is only slightly larger than the earth because of its extreme compactness. According to the theory first proposed by the British physicist R. H. Fowler, all atoms in the interior of white dwarfs are completely crushed, forming a mixture of free electrons and naked atomic nuclei. The calculations carried out by an Indian astrophysicist, S. Chandrasekhar, led to a unique mathematical relation between the white dwarfs mass, their radius, and the amount of hydrogen contained in their material.

The mass of Sirius B, which could easily be estimated by applying Kepler's laws to the Sirius A and B system, was found to be 95 per cent of the mass of the sun. But how does one measure the radius of a distant star which looks like a point even through the strongest telescope? This can be done on the basis of Einstein's general theory of relativity, which states that all physical processes are slowed down by strong gravitational fields. On the surface of the compact body of Sirius B the gravitational potential is indeed very large, and one would expect that the vibrations of all atoms would be slowed down quite considerably, thus resulting in an appreciable shift of all spectral lines toward the red end of the spectrum. It would be easy to observe that red shift if Sirius B were a single star. But unfortunately it always hangs around its master, the brilliant Sirius A, which is several thousand times brighter.

The difficult task of observing the spectral lines of Sirius B was undertaken in 1914 at the Mount Wilson Observatory by W. S. Adams, who did his best to cut off the bright light of Sirius A by shielding it with the edge of a razor blade. Fortunately, at that time the distance between the two components of Sirius was comparatively large, so that Adams succeeded in getting a tiny trace of the companion's spectral lines. From the measured red shift, it followed that the radius of Sirius B is 0.023 times the radius of the sun, and Chandrasekhar's formula indicated a hydrogen content of about 35 per cent.

Here the matter rested until 1939, when the carbon cycle and H-H reactions were introduced for the explanation of the energy production in stars. When one applied the formulae for the rates of the thermonuclear reactions to Sirius B, it became immediately clear that it could not contain any hydrogen at all, since even a small percentage of hydrogen would boost the rate of energy production to an incredibly high value. Thus nuclear physicists insisted that the radius of Sirius B must be at least three times smaller than would follow from Adams' observations. On the other hand, astronomers insisted that the observations must have been correct and that the nuclear physicists had made some mistake in their calculations. The natural thing would have been, of course, to repeat Adams' measurements of the red shift, but at that time Sirius B was so close to its brilliant master that the task was hopeless. And it was only quite recently, when the two components of Sirius again became separated by a more reasonable distance, that the measurements were repeated by a Soviet astronomer, Klim Beloborodov, with the result that the radius of Sirius B proved to be really 0.023 (and not 0.008) of the radius of the sun, as was required by the arguments based on thermonuclear reactions.

A more general problem than the transformations of

light elements and the energy production within the stars
was presented by the abundance of all chemical elements
in the universe. In the 1940s it was believed, not quite
correctly, that the universe as a whole is chemically homogeneous, and that the relative abundance of different elements was fairly well represented by the constitution of
our sun, the neighboring stars, and the interstellar material. About 99 per cent of matter was assumed to be
formed by hydrogen and helium in nearly equal quantities (by weight), the remaining 1 per cent being ac-
counted for by heavier elements in amounts decreasing
with increasing atomic weight. It was natural to assume
that the observed universal abundances of chemical ele-

*The relative motion of Sirius A and Sirius B, with ar-
rows indicating the epochs of Adams' and Beloborodov's
observations.*

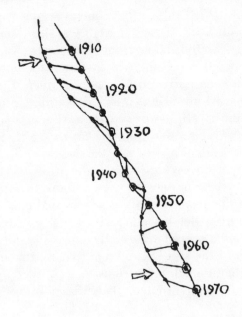

ments do not result from the nucleosynthesis within the individual stars, which would lead to a great variety of chemical constitution, but go back to the early "prestellar" state of the universe, when matter was distributed completely homogeneously through the entire space.

According to Friedmann's original theory of the expanding universe, it must have started with a "singular state" at which the density and temperature of matter were practically infinite. No atoms or even atomic nuclei could have existed at that time, and everything must have been broken into protons, neutrons, and electrons merged into the ocean of high energy radiation. I like to call that mixture "Ylem," since *Webster's Dictionary* defines this word as "the first substance from which the elements were supposed to be formed." As the universe was expanding and cooling, protons and neutrons must have started to stick together, forming the deuterons, i.e., the nuclei of heavy hydrogen. Further aggregations must have led to the heavier and heavier nuclei, resulting finally in the presently observed abundances of various chemical elements. Thus, knowing the probabilities of neutron-capture by different nuclei, one should be able to calculate the expected abundances of various atomic species and to compare them with the observed data. The probability of a neutron being captured by various nuclei had been measured in the Los Alamos Atomic Energy (Manhattan) Project, and after World War II the data were just in the process of being declassified.

And in 1948 I had just the right young man to do the job. He was Ralph Alpher, a graduate student of George Washington University, who was looking for a topic to work on for his Ph.D. thesis. Thus things started and went on smoothly. Alpher worked on war problems in the Applied Physics Laboratory (Navy Contract) in Silver Spring, Maryland, a suburb of Washington, D.C., where I was a consultant, so that the "formation of chemical elements" took place behind guarded gates. Early in the work we were joined by another APL employee, Robert Herman, a Princeton physics graduate who injected a lot of spirit into it.

Considering the behavior of the expanding universe during the very early stages of its existence, it was easy to conclude that at that time thermal radiation was playing a much more important role than that of the material particles. In fact, the mass density of radiation (according to the $M = E/c^2$ law of Einstein) must have been much larger than the combined mass of all material particles. From these conditions emerged a simple law for the temperature changes of the universe. At the age of 1 second, the universe must have had a temperature of 25,000,000,000 degrees, and as it grew older its temperature decreased as the square root of its age.

Alpher calculated that, in order to get a reasonable amount of heavier elements, one had to assume that the density of matter at the age of 1 second was about equal to the density of atmospheric air and decreased as the 1.5 power of the age. Extrapolating from the early days of the universe to the present time, we found that during the eons which had passed, the universe must have cooled to about 5 degrees above the absolute temperature. This was cool enough not to contradict the well-known coolness of interstellar and intergalactic space today. But it was a pleasant surprise when in 1965 A. A. Penzias and R. W. Wilson of Bell Telephone Laboratories, looking for something else, noticed an isotropic radiation of a wave length of 7.2 cm, which could correspond to thermal radiation at a temperature of about 3 degrees absolute.

Having heard of that discovery, R. H. Dicke, P. J. Peebles, P. C. Roll, and D. T. Wilkerson of Princeton University immediately interpreted the observed radiation as

*A composite picture of Robert Herman, George Gamow*
*(as a genie coming out of a bottle of ylem), and Ralph*
*Alpher, from photographs taken in 1949.*

the remnants of the primordial heat of many billion degrees that existed during the early days of the universe
and had cooled down to a miserable few degrees as a result of the gradual expansion of the universe over the period of some ten billion years.

The observations of the aforementioned authors, as well

as of many others who followed suit, established almost beyond any doubt that one deals here with the cooled-down primordial radiation which must have existed during "the days of creation." This finding gave a new impulse for the theoretical studies of the history of the expanding universe and is bound to lead to a better understanding of the important processes of the formation of galaxies and stars.

A few years later, in 1954, I made an extravagant deviation into the field of biological sciences. This was the year when the American biologist James Watson and the British crystallographer Francis Crick succeeded in constructing the correct model of the molecule of deoxyribonucleic acid (DNA), the basic genetic substance of all living organisms. This discovery earned for them, along with M. H. F. Wilkins of London, the 1962 Nobel Prize in Physiology and Medicine. The story of DNA has recently become quite familiar to the intelligent reading public through a somewhat controversial book, *The Double Helix,* written by James Watson.

After reading the Watson-Crick paper, published in *Nature* of May 1953, which explains how hereditary information is stored in DNA molecules in the form of a sequence of four different kinds of simple atomic groups known as "bases" (adenine, guanine, thyamine, and cytosine), I started to wonder how this information is translated into the sequence of *twenty* amino acids which form protein molecules. A simple idea which occurred to me was that one can "get 20 out of 4" by counting the number of all possible *triplets* formed out of four different entities. Consider, for example, a pack of playing cards in which we pay attention only to the suit of the card. How many triplets all of the same sort can one get? Four, of course: three hearts, three diamonds, three spades, and three

clubs. How many triplets with two cards of the same suit,
and one different? Well, we have four choices for the pair,
and, once we have made the choice, three choices for the
third card. Thus we have $4 \times 3 = 12$ possibilities. In addition we have four triplets with all three cards different.
Well, $4 + 12 + 4 = 20$, and that is exactly the number of
amino acids we want.

Here is a short description of the further development
of the coding theory, taken from an article by F. H. C.
Crick, "The Genetic Code—Yesterday, Today, and Tomorrow" (*Cold Spring Harbor Symposium,* Volume XXXI,
1966):

> The idea of coding was greatly helped by knowledge of
> the structure of DNA, published in 1953. Its simplicity
> excited many people, including the cosmologist George
> Gamow. An abbreviated account of Gamow's work first
> appeared in a short letter to *Nature* in 1954, and this was
> followed by a longer account in the *Proceedings of the
> Royal Danish Academy.* I am the proud possessor of one
> of the early drafts of this paper, then entitled "Protein
> Synthesis by DNA Molecules," the authors of which are
> G. Gamow and C. G. H. Tompkins! [2] (Gamow once told
> me that he submitted this paper to the "Proceedings of
> the National Academy" but they rather objected to the
> imaginary Mr. Tompkins as an author and for this reason
> it was eventually published by the Royal Danish Acad-
> emy, although with Gamow as sole author.) The paper is
> based on the idea that protein synthesis takes place on the
> surface of double-helical DNA and that the base sequence
> on the inside of the structure forms a series of cavities,
> each of which is specific for one of the amino acids. It is
> not stated in detail how the amino acids recognize these
> cavities, but the suggestion is fairly clear that they do so

[2] C. G. H. Tompkins, the hero of *Mr. Tompkins in Wonderland, Mr.
Tompkins Explores the Atom,* and *Mr. Tompkins Inside Himself,* is a
bank clerk with an insatiable curiosity about science.

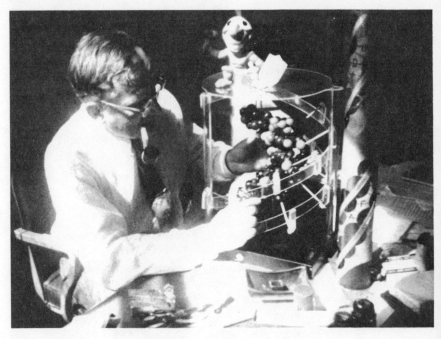

*Building a DNA model in 1954.*

by the side chains fitting in stereo-chemically, without any
assistance from special enzymes.

Gamow was concerned that the units in an extended
polypeptide chain are separated by only about 3.6 or 3.7 Å,
and for this reason his code was of the overlapping
type. Concerning the number of amino acids, he says that
this "is usually taken as twenty, although actually there
may be a few more." In fact, his Table I lists 25. The first
20 includes both cystine and cystcic acid (*sic*) and also hy-
droxproline, but not asparagine and glutamine. The
number is made up to 25 by the inclusion of norvaline,
hydroxyglutamic acid, and canine (whatever that is). It

was when we first saw this list, I think in the summer of
1953, that Watson and I, sitting in the Eagle at Cambridge, drew up the standard list of twenty which we have
today.

The importance of Gamow's work was that it was really
an abstract theory of coding, and was not cluttered up
with a lot of unnecessary chemical details, although his
basic idea that the double-stranded DNA was the tem-
plate for protein synthesis was, of course, quite wrong.
What he did realize clearly was that an overlapping code
put restrictions on the amino acid sequences, and that it
should be possible to prove, or at least disprove, various
overlapping codes by studying known amino acid sequences.

It was at about this time that Gamow founded that
strange organization, the RNA Tie Club. This was a
club, limited to 20 members (one for each amino acid), of
people who were interested in coding problems. It was
not a truly representative group of all those in the field,
but rather a haphazard collection of Gamow's friends.
There were also supposed to be four honorary members,
one for each of the four bases, though I do not think that
more than two of these were ever elected. The club had a
special tie, designed by Gamow and made by a haber-
dasher in Los Angeles, and each member was supposed to
have a tie-pin with the abbreviation for his own amino
acid marked on it. I have the tie, but I do not remember
ever having had a tie-pin.

If there really was a one-to-one correlation between 20
base-triplets and 20 amino acids, it should have been possible to find it from the known amino-acid sequences in
various proteins. But the data on protein sequences existing at that time were very meager, and the work was just
as difficult as breaking a secret military code on the basis
of just a couple of short messages supplied by the spies.
Since at that time I was consultant to the United States
Navy Department in Washington, D.C., I went to my

commanding admiral and asked if the problem could be given to a top-secret cryptographic group that was credited with breaking the Japanese code. As a result, three men appeared in my office at George Washington University and, without giving their names, told me that Admiral So-and-So had sent them. One of them had a beard, and I am still not sure that it was not an artificial one.

I gave them the problem, and within a few weeks they informed me that it has no solution. The same conclusion was reached by my biological friends: Martynas Yčas, originally from Lithuania, and Sidney Brenner, originally from South Africa. This excluded the possibility of an overlapping code and eliminated any simple way of finding the correlation on the basis of pure theory. Experimentalists went to work with their test tubes and centrifuges, and by 1964 M. W. Nirenberg and his co-workers from the National Institutes of Health in Bethesda, Maryland, had the problem licked. The solution looks considerably less elegant than the simple theoretical correlation which I had originally visualized, but it has the indisputable advantage of being correct, elegant or inelegant.

## MILITARY CONSULTATIONS

There is very little to say about my consultation work for the armed forces of the United States during World War II. It would have been, of course, natural for me to work on nuclear explosions, but I was not cleared for such work until 1948, after Hiroshima. The reason was presumably my Russian origin and the story I had told freely to my friends (and have told again in this book) of having been a colonel in the field artillery of the Red Army at the age of about twenty.

Thus I was very happy when I was offered a consultantship in the Division of High Explosives in the Bureau of

Ordnance of the U.S. Navy Department. This work did not interfere with my lectures and purely scientific research at George Washington University, since the university granted me permission to spend one day a week working for the Navy. I used it as two half-days weekly, working on Tuesday and Friday afternoons in an office at the old Navy Building on Constitution Avenue. The problems were mostly concerned with the propagation of shock and detonation waves in various conventional high explosives, and the discontinuous transitions from shock into detonation. My co-worker Dr. R. Finkelstein and I produced a long report on that subject which is now probably declassified and available in the archives of the Navy Department.

A more interesting activity during that time was my periodic contact with Albert Einstein, who, along with other prominent experts such as John von Neumann, served as a consultant for the High Explosive Division. Accepting this consultantship, Einstein stated that because of his advanced age he would be unable to travel periodically from Princeton to Washington, D.C., and back, and that somebody must come to his home in Princeton, bringing the problems with him. Since I happened to have known Einstein earlier, on nonmilitary grounds, I was selected to carry out this job. Thus on every other Friday I took a morning train to Princeton, carrying a briefcase tightly packed with confidential and secret Navy projects. There was a great variety of proposals, such as exploding a series of underwater mines placed along a parabolic path that would lead to the entrance of a Japanese naval base, with "follow up" aerial bombs to be dropped on the flight decks of Japanese aircraft carriers. Einstein would meet me in his study at home, wearing one of his famous soft sweaters, and we would go through all the proposals, one by one. He approved practically all of them, saying, "Oh

yes, very interesting, very, very ingenious," and the next
day the admiral in charge of the bureau was very happy
when I reported to him Einstein's comments.

After the business part of the visit was over, we had
lunch either at Einstein's home or at the cafeteria of the
Institute for Advanced Study, which was not far away, and
the conversation would turn to the problems of astrophysics and cosmology. In Einstein's study there were always
many sheets of paper scattered over his desk and on a
nearby table, and I saw that they were covered with tensor
formulae which seemed to pertain to the unified-field
theory, but Einstein never spoke about that. However, in
discussing purely physical and astronomical problems he
was very refreshing, and his mind was as sharp as ever.

I remember that once, walking with him to the institute, I mentioned Pascual Jordan's idea of how a star can
be created from nothing, since at the point zero its negative gravitational mass defect is numerically equal to its
positive rest mass. Einstein stopped in his tracks, and,
since we were crossing a street, several cars had to stop to
avoid running us down. I will never forget these visits to
Princeton, during which I came to know Einstein much
better than I had known him before.

My other part-time activity for the High Explosive Division had an experimental character and pertained to the
"dent sensitivity" of various explosives, i.e., the depend-
ence on the kinetic energy of the falling hammer. These
experiments were done in the Navy yards on the Potomac
River, in collaboration with a high-explosives expert. In
the course of those studies we made a very interesting discovery. It occurred to me that one could achieve very high
compression by producing a detonation wave that con-
verged at a point, and it became clear that such a conver-
gent detonation wave could be formed by combining two
explosives with different propagation velocities of the det-

onation process. Simple mathematics showed that, in order to achieve this effect, the boundary between the two explosives must be a section of an Archimedes spiral.

After that idea was approved by Einstein, it was decided to test a two-dimensional model at Indian Head, the Navy proving grounds on the Potomac River. However, Indian Head did not have the facilities for investigating a three-dimensional case, and it was decided to give that problem to a large high-explosives factory in Pittsburgh, which had a contract with the Bureau of Ordnance. But when I showed the drawing of the device to a man from Pittsburgh, he made a long face and said that his company could not undertake that task and refused to answer my question, "Why not?" On the next day my project was moved from the top of the priority list to the bottom, and I suddenly realized what was being worked on at a mysterious place in New Mexico with the address: P.O. Box 1663, Santa Fe. Years later, when I was finally cleared for work on the A-bomb and went to Los Alamos, I learned that my guess had been correct.

To my Navy consultation period also belonged the trip to Bikini for the first A-bomb test, but I was an outsider stationed on a submarine tender and my task was to study the effect of the shock wave on the surface structures of the target ships. But nevertheless, the expedition was very interesting and exciting.

After participating in the Task Force I operation, I began to work for the Army, becoming a consultant in the Army's Operation Research Office at Johns Hopkins University on Connecticut Avenue, one mile north of the D.C. line. The problems here were quite different, and I spent my time in developing the theory of war games, mostly analyzing battles between tanks. The game started with a simple 20-by-20-inch checkerboard with twenty blue and twenty red tanks (bought in a five-and-ten-cent store), which were moved according to the rules of the game. Some of the four hundred squares were painted yellow (open fields) and some green (wooded areas), and a tank on a green square always demolished an enemy tank on an adjacent yellow field. If two opposing tanks were located on neighboring green fields, there was no battle. If both were on neighboring yellow fields, the outcome of the battle was decided by tossing a coin. This simple scheme soon developed into a game of immense complexity, with two electronic computers handling the tactics of opposing forces.

More extensive was my relationship with the Los Alamos Scientific Laboratory after 1948, when a security

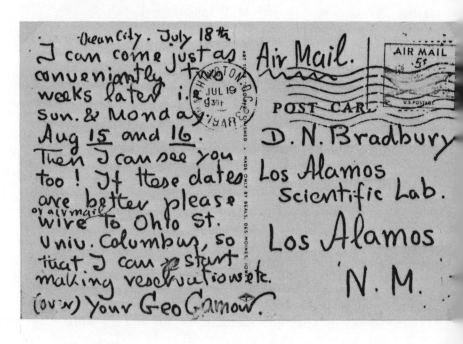

*Edward Teller (drawn by the author) and Stanislaw Ulam (drawn by Shatzi Davis) of the Los Alamos Scientific Laboratory.*

clearance was granted to me. I reproduce a postcard to Dr. Norris Bradbury, the Director of Los Alamos Scientific Laboratory, which represented my official acceptance of the invitation to come to Los Alamos for work on the fusion bomb. Another two drawings are essentially campaign posters. The first one shows the somewhat exaggerated faces of my good friends Edward Teller and Stanislaw Ulam, who are known as the mother and father of the H-bomb, and the second pertains to the era when President Truman was still hesitating whether to say yes or no to the development of the hydrogen bomb. Well, so much about military activities.

## POPULARIZATION OF SCIENCE

Apart from three mathematical treatises on the theory of the atomic nucleus, I have also written twenty books on science for the layman. I am often asked how I started to popularize science, and I really do not know the correct answer. Probably it is because I love to see things in a clear and simple way; trying to simplify them for myself, I learned how to do so for others. In any case, while I was still a student I liked to deliver popular lectures on complicated scientific subjects, and also from time to time wrote articles in popular and semi-popular scientific magazines. That is probably why, sometime in 1937, I wrote my first "Mr. Tompkins" story, in which I tried to explain the complicated ideas of the curved and expanding space of the universe by grossly exaggerating the effects so as to make them easily visualized by the man on the street. For the man on the street—curious, intelligent, but ignorant—I used a bank clerk, I really do not remember why. I called him Mr. Tompkins, a name which, for some reason, sounds a little funny to me. This was the name of a graduate student of mathematics whom I met in Ann Arbor during my first visit to the United States; he is now in charge of the electronic computer machines at the University of California at Los Angeles and I have seen him there a few times while visiting that institution. Why the name Tompkins sounded somewhat funny to me while, for example, Thompson does not, I do not know, and it really does not matter. Then, of course, I had to introduce a conventional white-bearded professor who explains to Mr. Tompkins the strange things he observes. The story was called "A Toy Universe," and I sent it to *Harper's Magazine,* which, I was told, publishes sophisticated articles. The manuscript was returned with a rejection slip, and I sent it out again to *The Atlantic*

*Monthly, Coronet,* and a few other magazines, with no
more success. So I put the manuscript in a drawer of my
desk and forgot about it.

In May of 1938 I went to Poland to attend a conference
on "New Theories in Physics" at the Pilsuzki University
in Warsaw, organized by the International Institute of Intellectual Cooperation, which was, I think, somehow connected with the League of Nations. The conference was
attended by Niels Bohr and Christian Møller from Denmark, Sir Arthur Eddington and Sir Charles Darwin from
England, Paul Langevin and Louis Brillouin from France,
and Eugene Wigner, John von Neumann, Samuel Goudsmit, and me from the United States. It promised to be
rather interesting.

Once, between the meetings, I was sitting with Sir
Charles in an outdoor café, sipping *miod* (a kind of beer
made of honey), and the conversation turned to the popularization of science. I told him about my fiasco with what
I thought was a very nice popular article, and he made a
suggestion.

"If you still have the manuscript," he said, "send it to a
man named C. P. Snow who edits a magazine called *Discovery* for Cambridge University Press. He himself tries
to popularize science, and I am sure will be interested in
your effort."

Thus, when I returned to Washington, I fished the old
manuscript from my desk and mailed it to England. The
next week I received a cable from Cambridge: "Your article will be published next issue. Send more. Snow." Well,
this was the beginning, and one Mr. Tompkins article followed another in the pages of *Discovery*.

About half a year later I received almost simultaneously
two letters. One was from Ronald Mansbridge, the manager of the American branch of Cambridge University
Press, suggesting that the Mr. Tompkins stories in *Discov-*

*ery*, with some additional material to boost the volume, should be published in book form; thus appeared my first popular book, *Mr. Tompkins in Wonderland.*[3] Another letter was from Pascal Covici, a senior editor of The Viking Press, asking me to write a book for them; this resulted in *The Birth and Death of the Sun.*[4]

These two houses have remained my major publishers, even though I have occasionally written books for other publishers, as, for example, *Matter, Earth, and Sky,* the college text on physical sciences, for Prentice-Hall.

The publication of my third Mr. Tompkins book, in which he investigates the field of biology, was associated with great changes in my personal life, including a divorce from my first wife, Rho. In the summer of 1953, when the book was published I had to go to England to attend a joint meeting of the American, Canadian, and British Armies' operational analysts, in Shrivenham War College. I was sailing in August for England on the then newly built ocean liner the *United States,* and Ronald Mansbridge was planning to see me off at the New York docks and to present me with the first copy of the book, *Mr. Tompkins Learns the Facts of Life,*[5] and a triangular bottle of Haig & Haig. To my surprise, instead of Mansbridge, there appeared on board a good-looking woman who introduced herself as Barbara Perkins, the publicity manager at Cambridge University Press. She handed me the copy of my book and the bottle of Haig & Haig, explaining that Ron-

[3] Updated versions of this title and of *Mr. Tompkins Explores the Atom* are now available in *Mr. Tompkins in Paperback* (London and New York: Cambridge University Press, 1965).

[4] To replace this book when it became obsolete, I wrote *A Star Called the Sun,* published by The Viking Press in 1964.

[5] To reflect the recent revolutionary developments in biology, I collaborated with my friend and former co-worker on genetic problems, Martynas Yčas, a professor of microbiology at the Medical Center of New York State University, on *Mr. Tompkins Inside Himself,* published by The Viking Press in 1968.

*Visiting the Taj Mahal with Barbara.*

ald had gone home because he had to be present at the
first performance of a high-school play in which his young
daughter was taking part. Before Miss Perkins had to go
ashore, I learned from her that she was responsible for the
successful promotion of my book.

During the years that followed I saw Barbara each time

I visited New York, taking her to dinner at Russian restaurants, to the movies, and so on. And in the fall of 1958, I asked her to be my wife. She arrived in Denver in October, and I drove with her to a justice of the peace in Estes Park to go through all necessary formalities, and on the way back we stopped at the Foothills Restaurant in Lyons for dinner and a celebration. We had some martinis before dinner and some champagne after it (or vice versa), and then drove back to Boulder. About halfway home, I noticed in my rear-view mirror the blinking red light of a car following me. I pulled to the curb, and a friendly-looking highway patrolman came to the window of my car.

*Feeding deer in Nara, Japan.*

"Was I doing something wrong, Officer?" I asked.

"Yes, you were going slightly above the speed limit."

"I am sorry, Officer," I said, "but, you see, we were just married."

"I want to see your license," said the patrolman.

"Here it is!" I said, and handed him the freshly signed marriage certificate, which, rolled up and tied with a pink ribbon, was resting on the seat between me and my wife.

"No, no!" she exclaimed. "He wants to see your *driving* license!"

I obliged, and after inspecting both documents the patrolman returned them to me, saying with a smile, "Well, you may drive on, but please slow down by some five miles. Congratulations, anyway!"

Well, this was the first (and I hope the last) speeding violation in all my driving career.

Do I enjoy writing books on popular science? Yes, I do. Do I consider it my major vocation? No, I do not. My major interest is to attack and to solve the problems of nature, be they physical, astronomical, or biological. But to "get going" in scientific research one needs an inspiration, an idea. And good and exciting ideas do not occur every day. When I do not have any new ideas to work on, I write a book; when some fruitful idea for scientific pursuit comes, writing lags. In any case, as I have said, I have published altogether twenty books on popular science, with two more in the making: a new one on cosmology, and this present autobiography. The popular books earned me the 1956 Kalinga Prize for the popularization of science (awarded by UNESCO), which resulted in a very interesting and pleasant lecture trip to India and Japan. If one includes the three treatises on nuclear physics, it will be twenty-five books, which is plenty for a lifetime. I do not plan to write any more books. One of the reasons

*Lecturing in Tokyo in 1959.*

is that I have written about practically everything I know. But there is a remote chance that I may publish a cookbook or a manual on big-game hunting.

People often ask me how I write books that are so successful. Well, it is a deep secret, so deep that I do not know the answer myself!

# A Brief Chronological Outline
# of George Gamow's Personal
# and Professional Life

| | |
|---|---|
| 1904 | Born, March 4, Odessa, Russia |
| 1922–1923 | Student at Novorossia University, Odessa |
| 1923–1929 | Student at University of Leningrad |
| 1928–1929 | Fellow of Theoretical Physics Institute of the University of Copenhagen |
| 1929–1930 | Rockefeller Fellow, Cambridge University |
| 1930–1931 | Fellow of Theoretical Physics Institute of the University of Copenhagen |
| 1931 | Married Lyubov Vokhminzeva ("Rho"); divorced 1956 |

| | |
|---|---|
| 1931–1933 | Professor, University of Leningrad |
| 1933–1934 (winter and spring) | Fellow of Pierre Curie Institute, Paris; Visiting Professor, University of London |
| 1934 (summer) | Lecturer, University of Michigan |
| 1934 (fall)–1956 | Professor, George Washington University, Washington, D.C. |
| 1935 | Son, Rustem Igor, born |
| 1954 | Visiting Professor, University of California, Berkeley |
| 1956 | Awarded Kalinga Prize by UNESCO for popularization of science |
| 1956–1968 | Professor, University of Colorado |
| 1958 | Married Barbara Perkins ("Perky") |
| 1965 (fall) | Overseas Fellow, Churchill College, Cambridge University |

# Publications
# by George Gamow

BOOKS[1]

M   *The Constitution of Atomic Nuclei and Radioactivity*. Oxford,
     England: Clarendon Press, 1931

M   *Structure of Atomic Nuclei and Nuclear Transformations*.
     Oxford, England: Clarendon Press, 1937

     *Mr. Tompkins in Wonderland*. London: Cambridge Univer-
     sity Press, 1939

     *The Birth and Death of the Sun*. New York: The Viking Press,
     1940

     *Biography of the Earth*. New York: The Viking Press, 1941

     *Mr. Tompkins Explores the Atom*. London: Cambridge Uni-
     versity Press, 1944

     *Atomic Energy in Cosmic and Human Life*. London: Cam-
     bridge University Press, 1947

     *One Two Three . . . Infinity*. New York: The Viking Press,
     1947

M   *Theory of Atomic Nucleus and Nuclear Energy Sources* (with
     C. Critchfield). Oxford, England: Clarendon Press, 1949

     *The Creation of the Universe*. New York: The Viking Press,
     1952

     *Mr. Tompkins Learns the Facts of Life*. London: Cambridge
     University Press, 1953

     *The Moon*. New York: Henry Schuman, 1953

     *Puzzle-Math* (with M. Stern). New York: The Viking Press,
     1958

[1] Books marked "M" are advanced monographs; those marked "C" are
college texts; the remainder are popular.

C    *Matter, Earth & Sky.* New York: Prentice-Hall, 1958
C    *Physics: Foundations & Frontiers* (with J. M. Cleveland). New
       York: Prentice-Hall, 1960
       *The Atom and Its Nucleus.* New York: Prentice-Hall, 1961
       *Biography of Physics.* New York: Harper & Row, 1961
       *Gravity* (Science Study Series). New York: Doubleday & Co.,
       1962
       *A Planet Called Earth.* New York: The Viking Press, 1963
       *A Star Called The Sun.* New York: The Viking Press, 1964
C    *Matter, Earth & Sky* (Revised edition). New York: Prentice-
       Hall, 1965
       *Mr. Tompkins in Paperback.* New York: Cambridge Univer-
       sity Press, 1965
       *Thirty Years That Shook Physics* (Science Study Series). New
       York: Doubleday & Co., 1966
       *Mr. Tompkins Inside Himself* (with Martinas Yčaš). New York:
       The Viking Press, 1967
       *My World Line: An Informal Autobiography.* New York: The
       Viking Press, 1970
C&M  *Basic Theories in Modern Physics* (with Richard Blade; in
       preparation for Academic Press)

ARTICLES[1]

    "Zur Wellentheorie der Materie," with D. Ivanenko. *Zeit-
       schrift für Physik,* Sonderabdruck Band 39, Heft 10, 11
    "Anomale Dispersion an den Linien der Hauptserie des
       Kaliums (Verhältnis der Dispersionskonstanten des roten und
       violetten Dubletts)," with W. Prokofiev. *Zeitschrift für
       Physik,* Sonderabdruck Band 44, Heft 11, 12
    "Zur Quantentheorie des Atomkernes." *Zeitschrift für Physik,*
       Sonderabdruck Band 51, Heft 3, 4
    "Zur Quantenmechanik des radioaktiven Kerns," with F. G.
       Houtermans. *Zeitschrift für Physik,* Sonderabdruck Band 52,
       Heft 7, 9
    "Zur Quantentheorie der Atomzertrümmerung." *Zeitschrift für
       Physik,* Sonderabdruck Band 52, Heft 7, 8
    "Bemerkung zur Quantentheorie des radioaktiven Zerfalls."
       *Zeitschrift für Physik,* Sonderabdruck Band 53, Heft 7, 8
    "Quantum Theory of Nuclear Disintegration." *Nature,* Novem-
       ber 24, 1928
    "Discussion on the Structure of Atomic Nuclei." *Proceedings
       of the Royal Society A,* Vol. 123

[1] Articles marked "P" can be considered popular articles.

"Successive Alpha-Transformations." *Nature,* April 20, 1929

"Mass Defect Curve and Nuclear Constitution." *Proceedings of the Royal Society A,* Vol. 126

"Über die Struktur des Atomkernes." *Physik,* Vol. 30

"Artificial Disintegration by Alpha-Particles," with J. Chadwick. *Nature,* July 13, 1930

"Fine Structure of Alpha-Rays." *Nature,* September 13, 1930

"Übergangswahrscheinlichkeiten von angeregten Kernen," with M. Delbruck. *Zeitschrift für Physik,* Sonderabdruck Band 72, Heft 7, 8

"Über die Theorie des radioaktiven $\alpha$ Zerfalls, der Kernzertrümmerung, und die Anregung durch $\alpha$ Strahlen/und Physik." *Physikalische Zeitschrift,* Vol. 32, 1931

"Quantum Theory of Nuclear Structure." *Reale Accademia d'Italia,* October 1931

"Nuclear Alpha- and P-Levels." *Physikalische Zeitschrift der Sowjetunion,* Band 1, Heft 3, 1932

"Radioactive Disintegration and Nuclear Spin." *Nature,* March 26, 1932

"Outlines of the Development of the Studies on the Atomic Nucleus." *Uspekhi Fizicheskikh, Nauk* 12, 13

"Mechanism of $\gamma$ Excitation by $\beta$ Disintegration." *Nature,* January 14, 1933

"Nuclear Energy Levels." *Nature,* March 25, 1933

"Fundamental State of Nuclear Alpha-Particles." *Nature,* April 29, 1933

"L'Origine des Rayons et les Niveaux d'Énergie Nucléaires." *98000 Institut Solvay (Physique),* October 1933

"Internal Temperature of Stars," with L. Landau. *Nature,* October 7, 1933

"Les Noyaux Atomiques." *Annales de l'Institut H. Poincaré,* December 1933

"Les Diamètres Effectifs des Noyaux Radioactifs," with S. Rosenblum. *Comptes Rendus des Séances de l'Académie des Sciences,* December 18, 1933

"Nuclear Spin of Radioactive Elements." *Proceedings of the Royal Society A,* Vol. 146

"Empirische Stabilitätsgrenzen von Atomkernen." *Zeitschrift für Physik,* Sonderabdruck Band 89, Heft 9, 10

"Negative Protons and Nuclear Structure." *The Physical Review,* May 15, 1934

"Modern Ideas on Nuclear Constitution." *Nature,* May 19, 1934

"Über den heutigen Stand (20 Mai 1934) der Theorie des $\beta$ Zerfalls." *Physikalische Zeitschrift,* Vol. 35, 1934

"General Stability-Problems of Atomic Nuclei." *Papers and Discussions of the International Conference on Physics, London 1934*, Vol. I

"Isomeric Nuclei?" *Nature*, June 2, 1934

"A Sketch of the Growth of the Study of the Structure of the Atomic Nucleus." *Uspekhi Fizicheskikh*, Nauk 14

"The Negative Proton." *Nature*, May 25, 1935

"Nuclear Transformations and the Origin of the Chemical Elements." *Ohio Journal of Science*, Vol. 35, No. 5

"Selection Rules for the $\beta$ Disintegration," with E. Teller. *The Physical Review*, June 15, 1936

"Possibility of Selective Phenomena for Fast Neutrons." *The Physical Review*, June 15, 1936

"On The Probability of $\gamma$ Ray Emission," with F. Bloch. *The Physical Review*, August 1, 1936

"Some Generalizations of the Transformation Theory," with E. Teller. *The Physical Review*, February 15, 1937

"Über den heutigen (1 Juni 1937) Stand der Theorie des $\beta$ Zerfalls." *Physikalische Zeitschrift*, Vol. 38, 1937

"A Star Model with Selective Thermo-Nuclear Source." *The Astrophysical Journal*, March 1938

"Nuclear Energy Sources and Stellar Evolution." *The Physical Review*, April 1, 1938

"The Rate of Selective Thermonuclear Reactions," with E. Teller. *The Physical Review*, April 1, 1938

"The Problem of Stellar Energy," with S. Chandrasekhar and M. A. Tuve. *Nature*, May 28, 1938

"Tracks of Stellar Evolution." *The Physical Review*, June 1, 1938

"On the Neutron Core of Stars," with E. Teller. *The Physical Review*, June 1, 1938

"L'évolution des Étoiles du Point de Vue de la Physique Moderne." *Annales de l'Institut H. Poincaré*, July 1938

"Tentative Theory of Novae." *The Physical Review*, September 15, 1938

"Zur ammenfassander Bericht, Kernumwandlung als Energiequelle der Sterne." *Zeitschrift für Astrophysik*, Sonderabdruck Band 16, Heft 3

"The Energy-Producing Reaction in the Sun." *The Astrophysical Journal*, October 1, 1938

"The Expanding Universe and the Origin of the Great Nebulae," with E. Teller. *Nature*, January 21, 1939

"The Expanding Universe and the Origin of the Great Nebulae," with E. Teller. *Nature*, March 4, 1939

"The Shell Source Stellar Model," with C. L. Critchfield. *The Astrophysical Journal,* March 1939

"On the Origin of Great Nebulae," with E. Teller. *The Physical Review,* April 1, 1939

"Physical Possibilities of Stellar Evolution." *The Physical Review,* April 15, 1939

"Energy Production in Red Giants," with E. Teller. *The Physical Review,* April 15, 1939

"Evolution of Red Giants." *The Physical Review,* April 15, 1939

"Basic Principles of the New Mechanics." *Science Monthly,* Vol. 51

"Nuclear Reactions in Stellar Evolution." *Nature,* September 30 and October 7, 1939

"The Possible Role of Neutrinos in Stellar Evolution," with M. Schoenberg. *The Physical Review,* December 15, 1940

"Concerning the Origin of Chemical Elements." *Journal of the Washington Academy of Science,* Vol. 32

"Neutrinos vs. Supernovae." *Science Monthly,* Vol. 54

"Neutrino Theory of Stellar Collapse," with M. Schoenberg. *The Physical Review,* April 1, 1941

"Relative Importance of Different Elements for Neutrino Production." *The Physical Review,* April 1, 1941

P    "How Stars Are Born." *American Weekly,* June 22, 1941

P    "Many More Worlds like Ours?" *American Weekly,* January 4, 1942

"Contractive Evolution of Massive Stars." *The Astrophysical Journal,* November 1943

"On WC and WN Stars." *The Astrophysical Journal,* November 1943

"The Evolution of Contracting Stars." *The Physical Review,* January 1 and January 15, 1944

"Recent Progress in Astrophysics," with J. A. Hynek. *The Astrophysical Journal,* March 1945

"A Shell Source Model for Red Giant Stars," with G. Keller. *Review of Modern Physics,* Vol. 17

"Rotating Universe?" *Nature,* September 13, 1946

"Expanding Universe and the Origin of Elements." *The Physical Review,* October 1 and October 15, 1946

"Probability of Nuclear Meson-Absorption." *The Physical Review,* April 15, 1947

P    "Universal Spin." *Newsweek,* Vol. 28

"The Origin of Chemical Elements," with R. A. Alpher and H. Bethe. *The Physical Review,* April 1, 1948

P    "Sun's Atomic Fuel." *Science Illustrated,* Vol. 2

P    "Galaxies in Flight." *Scientific American,* July 1948
     "The Origin of Elements and the Separation of Galaxies."
     *The Physical Review,* August 18, 1948
P    "Origin of the Ice." *Scientific American,* October 1948
     "The Evolution of the Universe." *Nature,* October 30, 1948
     "Thermonuclear Reactions in the Expanding Universe," with
     R. A. Alpher and R. Herman. *The Physical Review,* November 1, 1948
P    "Reality of Neutrinos." *Physics Today,* Vol. 1 (3)
     "Mixed Types of Stellar Populations." *Nature,* November 20, 1948
P    "Near the End?" *Time,* Vol. 53
P    "Supernovae." *Scientific American,* December 1949
P    "Existence of the Neutrino." *Physikalische Blätter,* Heft 5
     "Problem of Red Giants and Cepheid Variables," with C. Longmire. *The Physical Review,* August 15, 1950
     "On the Stellar Dynamics of Spherical Galaxies," with J. Belzer and G. Keller. *The Astrophysical Journal,* January 1951
     "Hydrogen Exhaustion and Explosions of Stars." *Nature,* July 14, 1951
     "On Relativistic Cosmogony." *Review of Modern Physics,* Vol. 21
     "The Role of Turbulence in the Evolution of the Universe." *The Physical Review,* April 15, 1952
P    "Turbulence in Space." *Scientific American,* June 1952
P    "Start of Things." *Newsweek,* Vol. 39
     "Expanding Universe and the Origin of Galaxies." *Kongelige Danske Videnskabernes Selskab,* Vol. 27
     "Possible Relation Between DNA and the Protein Structures." *Nature,* February 13, 1954
P    "Modern Cosmology." *Scientific American,* March 1954
     "Turbulent Origin of Galaxies." *Proceedings of the National Academy of Sciences,* Vol. 40
     "Possible Mathematical Relation Between Deoxyribonucleic Acid and Proteins." *Kongelige Danske Videnskabernes Selskab,* Vol. 22
     "Topological Properties of Coiled Helical Systems." *Proceedings of the National Academy of Sciences,* Vol. 41
     "On Information Transfer from Nucleic Acids to Proteins." *Kongelige Danske Videnskabernes Selskab,* Vol. 22
     "Statistical Correlation of Protein and Ribonucleic Acid Composition," with M. Yčas. *Proceedings of the National Academy of Sciences,* Vol. 41
P    "Information Transfer in the Living Cell." *Scientific American,* October 1955

"Nucleoproteins." Roundtable discussion. *Journal of Cellular Comparative Physiology*, Vol. 47, Suppl. 1

P "Evolutionary Universe." *Scientific American*, September 1956

"The Problem of Information Transfer from the Nucleic Acids to Proteins," with A. Rich and M. Yčas. *Advances of Biological and Medical Physics*, Vol. IV

"Physics of the Expanding Universe." *Vistas in Astronomy*. London and New York: Pergamon Press, 1956, Vol. 2

P "A Rocket around the Moon," with Krafft A. Ehricke. *Scientific American*, June 1957

P "The Principle of Uncertainty." *Scientific American*, January 1958

P "The Creation of the Universe." *The Sewanee Review*, summer 1958

P "The Exclusion Principle." *Scientific American*, July 1959

P "The Heart on the Other Side." *University of Colorado Literary Magazine*, Vol. 72 (spring 1961)

P "Gravity." *Scientific American*, March 1961

"Negative Entropy and Photosynthesis," with W. Brittin. *Proceedings of the National Academy of Sciences*, Vol. 47

"Remarks on Lorentz Contraction." *Proceedings of the National Academy of Sciences*, Vol. 47

P Articles in *Encyclopaedia Britannica* (see *E.B.* index)

P Articles in *Encyclopedia Americana* (see *E.A.* index)

P "The Physical Sciences and Technology." *The Great Ideas Today*. Chicago: Encyclopaedia Britannica, Inc., 1962

P "Niels Bohr, the Man Who Explained the Atom." *Science Digest*, May 1963

P "What is Life?" *Transactions of the Bose Research Institute, Calcutta*, Vol. 24

P "Astronomy on Christmas Eve." *Boys' Life*

P "Epilogue. On Lunar Theory." *The Hopkins Manuscript* by R. C. Sheriff. New York: Macmillan, 1963

P "The Origin of Life." *Transactions of the Bose Research Institute, Calcutta*, Vol. 24

"Cosmological Theories of the Origin of Chemical Elements." *Perspectives in Modern Physics*. New York: Interscience Publishers, 1966

P Review of *Niels Bohr: The Man, His Science, and the World They Changed* by Ruth Moore. *The New York Times Book Review*, October 23, 1966

P Review of *Otto Hahn: A Scientific Autobiography*. New York *World-Journal-Tribune*, November or December 1966

"Does Gravity Change with Time?" *Proceedings of the National Academy of Sciences*, Vol. 57

"Surface Tension and the Contraction of Muscles." *Proceedings of the National Academy of Sciences*, Vol. 57

"Electricity, Gravity and Cosmology." *The Physical Review*, Letters, September 25, 1967

"Variability of Elementary Charge and Quasistellar Objects." *The Physical Review*, Letters, October 16, 1967

Addendum to the paper "Electricity, Gravity and Cosmology." *The Physical Review*, Letters, October 23, 1967

"Case of the Vanished Correlation in Statistics of Quasistellar Objects." *Nature*, November 4, 1967

"History of the Universe," and two "Letters to Phil." *Science*, Vol. 158

"Thermal Cosmic Radiation and the Formation of Protogalaxies," with R. A. Alpher and R. Herman. *Proceedings of the National Academy of Sciences*, Vol. 57

"On the Origin of Galaxies." *Properties of Matter under Unusual Conditions (Edward Teller 60th Birthday Volume)*. New York: John Wiley & Sons, Inc., Interscience Publishers, 1968

"Numerology of the Constants of Nature." *Proceedings of the National Academy of Sciences*, Vol. 58

"Observational Properties of the Homogeneous and Isotropic Expanding Universe." *The Physical Review*, Letters, June 3, 1968

"Naming the Units." *Nature*, August 1968

"A Possible Relation between Cosmological Quantities and the Characteristics of Elementary Particles," with R. Alpher. *Proceedings of the National Academy of Sciences*, Vol. 61

# Index